## "I was ready to battle him for you."

Christian murmured the words, fingers grazing the wet streak on her cheek. "To demonstrate how committed I am to being your ardent husband and a zealous father to Marc."

Such beautiful words from such a challenging and unpredictable man. Noelle couldn't decide whether to laugh or cry. She was still debating when Christian cupped her face in his hands and brought his lips to hers.

The delicious pressure of his kiss held her immobile with shock for several frantic heartbeats.

She tunneled impatient fingers into Christian's hair and pushed her greedy body hard against his. She craved a man's hands on her. To feel a little helpless as he tore her clothes off and had his way with her. And Christian had a knack for that sort of thing.

His fingers bit into her hips as she rocked against him, the ache between her thighs building. When she could stand it no longer, she cried out as pleasure lanced downward.

Christian buried his face in her neck, lips gliding over her skin. "I knew you'd come around."

An icy chill swept through her at his words. Noelle clenched her teeth and cursed her impulsiveness. She tensed her muscles and twisted away.

"I haven't come around to anything."

* * *

*Secret Child, Royal Scandal* is part of Cat Schield's Sherdana Royals trilogy

Dear Reader,

So many of you wanted Christian's story, and I'm glad to finally bring him to you. The three Alessandro brothers couldn't have been more different, and I was so excited to write about Christian because he's a bad boy with a weak spot for one particular lady.

The best part about writing is getting the chance to indulge in things I'm passionate about. In this story, it's castles, couture and the parent/child relationship. I loved exploring Christian's attempts to get to know his son and Noelle's concerns about what the future might hold for Marc if he became heir to the throne.

I hope you enjoy this third book in my Sherdana Royals series.

All the best,

*Cat Schield*

# SECRET CHILD, ROYAL SCANDAL

CAT SCHIELD

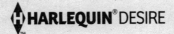

ISBN-13: 978-0-373-73455-9

Secret Child, Royal Scandal

Copyright © 2016 by Catherine Schield

**Printed in U.S.A.**

**Cat Schield** has been reading and writing romance since high school. Although she graduated from college with a BA in business, her idea of a perfect career was writing books for Harlequin. And now, after winning the Romance Writers of America 2010 Golden Heart® Award for Best Contemporary Series Romance, that dream has come true. Cat lives in Minnesota with her daughter, Emily, and their Burmese cat. When she's not writing sexy, romantic stories for Harlequin Desire, she can be found sailing with friends on the St. Croix River, or in more exotic locales, like the Caribbean and Europe. She loves to hear from readers. Find her at catschield.net. Follow her on Twitter, @catschield.

## Books by Cat Schield

### HARLEQUIN DESIRE

#### *The Sherdana Royals*

*Royal Heirs Required*
*A Royal Baby Surprise*
*Secret Child, Royal Scandal*

#### *Las Vegas Nights*

*At Odds with the Heiress*
*A Merger by Marriage*
*A Taste of Temptation*

Visit her Author Profile page at Harlequin.com, or catschield.net, for more titles!

To Renee and Mary K.
Thanks for all the happy hours and the
conversations that have kept me sane.

# One

Prince Christian Alessandro, third in line to the Sherdana throne, stood behind the current and future kings of Sherdana and glowered into the camera. No doubt he was ruining Nic and Brooke's fairy-tale wedding photos, but he didn't care. His last hope to remain a carefree bachelor for the rest of his life had been reduced to ashes the second his brother had gazed deep into his bride's starry eyes and pledged to love and honor her until the day he died.

Christian growled.

"Smiles everyone," the photographer cried, casting an anxious glance Christian's way. "This is our last photo of the complete wedding party. Let's make it count."

Despite his black mood, Christian shifted his features into less grim lines. He wasn't about to smile, but he could at least give his brother one decent photo. No matter how badly this marriage had disrupted his life, in the days to come he really would make an effort to be happy for Nic and Brooke. For today he'd simply don a mask.

"Let's set up over there." The photographer pointed to a small stone bridge that crossed a decorative creek.

The path beyond meandered toward the stables. Christian preferred his horsepower under the hood of a fast car, but he'd gladly take his twin nieces to visit their ponies just to get away. Bethany and Karina were old hands at being flower girls, this being their second royal wedding in four months, but being two-year-olds, they had a short attention span and were growing impatient with having to stand still for photos. Christian sympathized with them.

Since his accident five years earlier, he'd avoided cameras as much as possible. The burn scars that covered his right side—shoulder, neck and half of his cheek—had made him the least attractive Alessandro triplet. Not that it mattered much how he looked. His title, wealth and confirmed bachelor status made him a magnet for women.

Most women.

His gaze roamed over the multitude of assistants and palace staff required to keep the bridal party looking flawless and the photo shoot moving forward. Trailing the bride was a petite, slender woman with mink-brown hair and dual-toned brown eyes. Internationally renowned wedding dress designer Noelle Dubone had designed Brooke's dress as well as the one worn by Christian's sister-in-law, Princess Olivia Alessandro.

Born in Sherdana, Noelle had moved to Paris at twenty-two to follow her dream of becoming a fashion designer. She'd done moderately well until three years ago when she'd designed the wedding gown for the bride of Italian prince Paolo Gizzi. There'd been so much media coverage surrounding the nuptials that Noelle became an overnight success. Movie stars, European nobility and the very wealthy became eager for a Noelle Dubone original.

"Imagining your own wedding?" taunted a female voice from behind him.

Christian turned and shot his sister a sour look. Ariana was looking too smugly amused for Christian's taste.

"No." But the slim figure in blue-gray caught his eye again.

Noelle Dubone. The one woman in the world who'd come closest to taming the wildest Alessandro prince. He hadn't been worthy of her. She hadn't deserved to be treated badly by him. That he'd done it for her own good was what let him sleep at night.

"You should be," Ariana countered, looking stylish and carefree in a knee-length, full-skirted dress with puffy long sleeves. A fashion trendsetter, her wedding attire shimmered with gold embroidery and straddled the line between daring and demure with strategically placed sheer panels that showed off her delicate shoulders and hinted at more thigh than the formal occasion called for. "The future of the kingdom rests in your hands."

Christian grimaced. "Father's health has never been better and I don't see Gabriel dropping dead any time soon, so I suspect I will have time to choose a wife and get her pregnant."

Just the thought of it made him long for a drink. But as his mother had pointed out numerous times in the months since Nic had abdicated his responsibility to Sherdana by choosing to marry an American, Christian was no longer free to overindulge in liquor and women. The idea that he had to start walking the straight and narrow path after being the party prince all his life was daunting. He'd misstepped all his life. As youngest in the birth order, it was what he did.

Gabriel, as eldest, was the responsible one. The future king.

Nic, as middle son, was the forgotten one. He'd gone

off to America in his early twenties to become a rocket scientist.

Christian was the indulged youngest son. His antics had provided the paparazzi tabloid fodder since he was fourteen and got caught with one of the maids.

At twenty he'd been raising hell in London. He'd thrown the best parties. Drank too much. Spent money like it was being printed by elves, and when his parents cut off his funds, he'd started buying and flipping failing businesses. He didn't care about success. He just wanted to have fun.

At twenty-five several of his less prudent actions had blown up in his face, leaving him scarred and his heart shredded.

Now at thirty he was expected to give up his freedom for the crown.

"You only think you have time," Ariana countered. "Mother showed me the list of potential candidates. It's two-feet long."

"I do not need her help or anyone else's to find a wife."

"Neither did Gabriel and Nic and look how that turned out."

Gabriel had eloped five months earlier in a grand, romantic gesture that had rendered him blissfully happy, but by marrying a woman who could never have children, he'd left his two brothers holding short straws.

As the last born of the triplets, Christian had made it clear to Nic that it was his duty to step up next. In order for the Alessandro family to stay in power, one of the three princes needed to produce a son. But before Nic could begin looking for a potential bride from among Europe's noble houses or Sherdana's female citizenry, the beautiful American, Brooke Davis, had stolen his heart.

And with their wedding today, it all came down to Christian.

"I can find my own bride without Mother's help."

Ariana made a noise unfit for a princess. "You've already been through half the suitable single women in Europe.

"Hardly half."

"Surely there was one woman among *all* those you've spent time with who appeals to you."

"Appeals, yes." Christian resisted the urge to search for Noelle again. "But not one I want to spend the rest of my life with."

"Well, you'd better find one."

Christian ground his teeth together and didn't answer. He knew Ariana was right. The price one paid as a royal was to not always get to do as one liked. Gabriel had been lucky to choose Olivia to marry before he understood that he was in love with her. But right up until he and Olivia eloped, Gabriel had grappled with his duty to Sherdana versus following his heart's desire.

Nic had the same issue with Brooke. He'd known he needed to put her aside and marry a woman whose children could one day be king.

But in the end both men had chosen love over duty.

Which left Christian to choose duty.

One of the photographer's assistants came to fetch them for more pictures, putting an end to the conversation for the moment. Christian endured another tedious hour of being posed with his brothers, his sister, the king and queen, and various members of the wedding party. By the time the session was finished, he was ready to get drunker than he'd been in the five years since the accident that left him with a disfigured body to match his tarnished soul.

What stopped him from making a beeline for the bar was Noelle.

It seemed perfectly right to walk up behind her and slip

his arm around her waist. Christian dropped a kiss on her cheek the way he had a hundred times, a habit from the old days that used to speak to his strong affection for her. For a microsecond Noelle relaxed against him, accepting his touch as if no time or hurt had passed between them. Then she tensed.

"You look beautiful," he murmured in her ear.

She didn't quite jerk away from him, but she lacked her usual grace in her quick sideways step. "Thank you, Your Royal Highness."

"Walk with me." It was more a command than an invitation.

"I really shouldn't leave the party." She glanced toward the bride and groom as if hoping to spot someone who needed her.

"The photos are done. The bride has no further need for her designer. I'd like to catch up with you. It's been a long time."

"As you wish, Your Highness." To his annoyance, she curtsied, gaze averted.

The gardens behind the palace were extensive and scrupulously maintained under the queen's watchful eye. The plantings closest to the I-shaped structure that housed Sherdana's royal family were arranged in terms of design and color that changed with the seasons. This was the most photographed section of the garden, with its formal walkways and dramatic fountains.

Toward the back of the extensive acreage that surrounded the palace, the garden gave way to a wooded area. Christian guided her to a small grove of trees that offered plenty of shade. There would be more privacy there.

"You've done very well for yourself as a designer."

Christian hated small talk, and it seemed idiotic to attempt any with Noelle. But how did you begin a cordial conversation with an ex-lover who you'd once deliberately hurt even as you told yourself it was for her own good?

"I've been fortunate." Her polite demeanor contrasted with the impatience running through her tone. "Luck and timing."

"You neglected to mention talent. I always knew you'd be successful."

"That's very kind."

"I've missed you." The words came out of nowhere and shocked him. He'd intended to ply her with flirtatious compliments and make her smile at him the way she used to, not pour his heart out.

For the first time she met his gaze directly. His heart gave a familiar bump as he took in the striking uniqueness of her eyes. From a distance they merely looked hazel, but up close the greenish-brown around the edges gave way to a bright chestnut near the pupil. In the past, he'd spent long hours studying those colors and reveling in the soft affection in her gaze as they lingered over dinner or spent a morning in bed.

She gave her head a shake. "I'm sure that's not true."

"I might not have been the man for you, but that doesn't mean I didn't care," he told her, fingertips itching to touch her warm skin.

"Don't try to flatter me." The words held no heat. "I was a convenient bed for you to fall into after you were done partying. You came to me when you grew tired of your superficial crowd and their thoughtless behavior. And in the end, you pushed me out of your life as if two years together meant nothing."

*For your own good.*

"And look how you thrived. You moved to Paris and became an internationally famous designer." He sounded defensive, and that wasn't the tone he wanted to take with her.

"Is that what you think I wanted?" Her breath huffed out in a short burst that he might have taken for laughter if she hadn't been frowning. "Fame and fortune?"

No, it's what he'd wanted for her. "Talent like yours shouldn't go to waste."

"Do you want me to thank you?" she asked, her voice dripping with sarcasm.

During the time they were together, he'd been more honest with her than anyone else before or since. Not even his brothers had known of the demons that drove him. Maybe he trusted Noelle because they'd been friends before they became lovers. Her openness and gentle spirit had offered him a safe place to unload all his fears and doubts. And because of that, she'd gotten the full weight of his darkness.

"No."

"Then why are we having this conversation after five years of silence?"

Because once again he needed her solace and support. The pressure of fathering the future heir to Sherdana's throne was dredging up his worst qualities. She'd talked him through bouts of melancholy in the past.

"I need you."

Her expression reflected dismay. "I'm no longer that girl." Her tone heated as she continued. "And even if I was, I have other things in my life that will always take priority over a…" As if realizing what she'd been about to say to her prince, Noelle sucked in a giant breath and pulled her lips between her teeth. Her next words were polite, her tone tempered. "I am no longer in a position to be your *friend*."

She twisted the word *friend* into something ugly. Christian read her message loud and clear. She wanted nothing more to do with him. Not as his confidante, his champion or as his lover.

Before he could argue, she dropped another one of

those annoying curtsies. "Excuse me, Your Highness, but I should get back to the party."

Christian watched her vanish back along the path and marveled at how thoroughly he'd mucked up his most important act of selflessness. She was right to shut him down. He'd repeatedly demonstrated that he was nothing but trouble for her.

But after talking to her, he knew if he was going to get through the next few months of finding a wife and settling down to the job of producing the next heir to the throne, he was going to need a friend in his corner. And once upon a time, Noelle had been the only one he talked to about his problems.

He desperately wanted her support. And although she might not be on board with the idea at the moment, he was going to persuade her to give it.

The evening air accompanied Noelle into the small, functional kitchen of her comfortable rural cottage, bringing the earthy scents of fall with her. As much as she'd enjoyed her years in Paris, she'd missed the slower pace and wide-open spaces of the countryside. And an energetic boy like her son needed room to run.

She placed the tomatoes she'd picked on the counter. Her garden was reaching the end of its growing season, and soon she would collect the last of the squash, tomatoes and herbs. Autumn was her favorite season. The rich burgundy, gold and vivid greens of the hills around her cottage inspired her most unique designs. One downside to her success as a wedding-dress designer was that her color palate was limited to shades of white and cream with an occasional pastel thrown in.

"Mama!"

Before Noelle could brace herself, her dark-haired

son barreled into her legs. Laughing, she bent down and wrapped her arms around his squirmy little body. Like most four-years-olds he was a bundle of energy, and Noelle got her hug in fast.

"Did you have a good afternoon with Nana?" Noelle's mother lived with them and watched Marc after school while Noelle worked. She glanced at her mother without waiting for her son's response.

"He was a good boy," Mara Dubone said, her tone emphatic.

Noelle hoped that was true. In the past six months, Marc had grown more rambunctious and wasn't good at listening to his grandmother. Mara loved her grandson very much and defended him always, but it worried Noelle that her son was getting to be too much for her mother to handle.

"I was good." Marc's bronze-gold eyes glowed with sincerity and Noelle sighed.

She framed his face, surveyed the features boldly stamped by his father and gave him a big smile. "I'm so glad."

He had his father's knack for mischief as well as his charm. The thought caused Noelle a small pang of anxiety. Her encounter with Christian this afternoon had been unsettling. After almost five years of no contact, he'd finally reached out to her. That it was five years too late hadn't stopped her heart from thumping wildly in her chest.

"Why don't you go upstairs and brush your teeth," Mara said. "Your mama will come read to you, but she can't do that until you're in your pajamas and in bed."

"Yeah." With typical enthusiasm, Marc raced upstairs, his stocking feet pounding on the wood steps that led to the second floor.

"Was he really okay today?" Noelle asked as soon as she was alone with her mother.

Mara sighed. "He is a wonderful boy, but he has a lot of energy and needs a firm hand." Noelle's mother gave her daughter a sly grin. "What he needs is a man in his life who can channel some of that energy into masculine pursuits."

It wasn't the first time her mother had made this observation. Noelle nodded the way she always did. "Marc's friends are going fishing with their fathers next week. Phillip's dad offered to take Marc, as well. Perhaps I should take him up on his offer."

"That's not what I meant and you know it." Noelle's mother set her hands on her hips and shook her head. "You are not getting any younger. It's time you stopped pining for that prince of yours. It's been almost five years. You need to move on."

"I am not pining for Christian. And I have moved on. I have a thriving business that takes up most of my energy and a small boy who deserves his mother's full attention."

With a disgusted snort, Noelle's mother headed for the stairs. From above their heads came a series of loud thumps as Marc worked off his energy before bedtime.

Noelle walked back into the kitchen to turn off the light and then repeated the process in the dining room and living room before heading up to the bedrooms. For a moment she paused at the bottom of the stairs and listened to the sounds of her family. Her mother's low voice, patient and firm. Her son's clear tones, happy and dynamic.

A firm knock on her front door snapped Noelle out of her musing. She glanced at the clock over the mantel. Eight forty-five. Who could be visiting her at this hour?

Although her farmhouse sat on an acre of land, Noelle had never worried about her isolation. She had neighbors on all sides and they kept an eye on her and her family. Perhaps one of her goats had escaped again. She'd been having problems with the fence on the east side of their pasture.

Flipping on the light in the foyer, Noelle pulled the door open. Her smile died as she spotted the man standing outside her front door.

"Christian?"

Determination lit his gold eyes. While at his brother's wedding, she'd found it easy to discourage the arrogant prince who'd put his arm around her waist and boldly kissed her cheek.

"Good evening, Noelle."

Anxiety gripped her. She'd worked hard to keep her personal life private. Having Prince Christian Alessandro show up like this threatened that.

"What are you doing here?"

"We didn't get a chance to finish our conversation earlier."

Why was she surprised that after five years of no contact he would think she'd welcome his popping around with no warning the way he used to when they were together?

"It's almost nine o'clock."

"I brought some wine." He held up a bottle of her favorite red. *Damn the man for remembering.* He gave her a coaxing half grin. His eyes softened with the seductive glow she'd never successfully resisted. "How about letting me in."

She crossed her arms over her chest, refusing his peace offering. "I already told you. I'm not the same girl I was when we were together." She had said the exact same thing earlier that afternoon, but obviously he hadn't been listening. "You can't just show up here unannounced and think that I'm going to let you in." To warm her bed for a few hours.

"You're mad because I haven't called."

He was apologizing for not contacting her? "It's been five years." Half a decade of living had happened to her.

It took all her willpower not to shove him off her stoop and slam the door in his face.

"I know how long it's been. And I wasn't kidding earlier when I said I missed you. I'd like to come in and find out what your life is like now."

"I've been back in Carone for two years. Why now?"

"Talking with you today brought up a lot of great memories. We had something."

"The operative word being 'had.'" A tremor went through her as she remembered the feel of his fingers against her skin, working magic unlike anything she'd known before or since. "My life is wonderful. I'm happy and complete. There's no room for you or your drama."

"I'm not the same man I used to be, either."

From what she'd read about him over the years, she believed he'd changed, but it wasn't enough to invite him in. "What we did or didn't have in the past needs to stay there." She knew immediately that her words had been a mistake.

"Did or didn't have?" The light of challenge flared in his eyes. "You mean to stand there and deny that we were friends?"

Friends?

Is that how he'd thought of her as he made love to her for hours? When he'd told her he didn't like her going out after close with the guys from the café where she worked part-time and demanded that she stop? Friends? When he'd treated her more like his embarrassing secret?

Noelle realized her hands had clenched into fists at his declaration and tried to focus on relaxing. He was no less infuriating than on the day he'd told her they had no future and she should go to Paris and take the job at Matteo Pizzaro Designs.

"What do you want, Christian?" She asked the question in a flat, unfriendly tone that was intended to annoy him. It didn't.

"I never could get anything past you." He straightened, putting aside all attempt to charm her. Determination radiated from him. "Can I come in? I really do want to talk to you."

"It's late." From the floor above came the pounding of feet. Marc had grown impatient and would be coming to look for her any second. "Perhaps later this week. We could meet for coffee."

"I'd rather have a private dinner. Just you and me like the old days. Perhaps you could come to my place in the city? I have some things I'd like to discuss with you and I don't want to do so in public."

Bitterness gripped her. He'd never wanted to be seen out and about with her. She scrutinized his expression. He'd obviously come to her with an agenda. But she sensed what he had to say wasn't about her son. So far, her secret remained safe. If he'd known about Marc, he would have led with that. So, what was he up to?

"I'm afraid my evenings are booked." Spending time with her son was her greatest joy, and he was growing up so fast. She cherished her evenings with him and resented any intrusion. "Perhaps I could come to your office?"

There was thumping on the stairs as Marc jumped down each step, one by one. Noelle's heart hammered in time. She had to conclude the conversation with Christian before her son appeared.

"Call me. We can discuss this next week. Right now, I need to go." She started to shut the door, but Christian put out his hand and stopped it. Marc's feet thundered across the wood floor; he was coming closer. "Fine. I'll have dinner with you."

"Mama, where are you?"

Christian's eyes widened at the sound of Marc's voice. "You have a child?"

She could not let this happen. Noelle shifted to put her full weight against the door and get it closed.

"You have to leave."

"Marc, where are you?" She heard her mother coming down the stairs now and prayed that Mara could get to Marc before he came to investigate. "I told you your mother wouldn't read you a story unless you were in bed."

"I had no idea," Christian mused, his expression strangely melancholy.

"And now you see why my evenings are busy. So if you don't mind, I need to get my son to bed."

"Can I meet him?" The prince stared past Noelle into the home's interior.

"No." Hearing the snap in her voice, she moderated her tone. "It's his bedtime, and meeting someone new will stir him up. It's already difficult to settle him down enough to sleep."

"He sounds like me."

It was a remark anyone might have made. Noelle knew there was no subtext beneath Christian's comment, but she was hyper-secretive regarding the paternity of her son.

"Not at all."

"Don't you remember how much trouble you had getting me to sleep on the nights I stayed over?"

She ignored the jump in her pulse brought on by his wicked smile. What she remembered were long, delicious hours of lovemaking that left her physically drained and emotionally invigorated.

"This is a conversation for another time."

"Mama, who are you talking to?" Marc plastered himself against her hip and peered up at Christian.

Too late. She'd let Christian distract her with bittersweet

memories, and now he was about to discover what she'd zealously kept hidden from him all these years.

"This is Prince Christian," she told her son, heart breaking. "Your Highness, this is my son, Marc."

"*Your* son?" The prince regarded the four-year-old boy in silence for several seconds, his mouth set in a hard line. At last his cold eyes lifted to Noelle. "Don't you mean *our* son?"

# Two

Christian wanted to shove the door open and turn on the lights in the front entry so he could get a clearer look at the boy, but instinct told him it wouldn't change anything. This was his son.

"I don't have a father. Do I, Mama?" Marc glanced up at his mother, eyes worried as he took in her stricken expression.

"Of course you have a father," Noelle stated. "Everyone does. But not everyone's father is part of their life." She soothed a trembling hand over her son's dark head.

"And whose fault is that?" Christian's shock was fading, replaced with annoyance and grudging respect as he surveyed the boy—Noelle had called him Marc.

Tall for his age, which couldn't have been more than four and a half, he possessed the distinctive gold Alessandro eyes and wavy brown hair. Undaunted by Christian's keen scrutiny, the boy stared back, showing no apprehension, just unflinching hostility. And maybe a little curiosity, as well. Christian inclined his head in approval. A child of his would possess an inquisitive mind.

"We are not talking about this right now." Noelle glared at him. Motherhood had given her voice a sharp inflection that demanded immediate obedience. Almost immediately, however, her eyes widened as if she recalled that the man standing on her doorstep was a member of the royal family. Noelle modulated her tone. "Prince Christian, this is not a good time."

"I'm not leaving until I know what's going on."

"I'll make him go." Marc pushed past his mother and took up a fighter's stance, one foot back, fists up and ready to punch.

Christian didn't like how the situation was escalating, but he couldn't bring himself to back off. Too many questions bombarded him. Instead, he stared, belligerent and stubborn, into Noelle's lovely, troubled eyes until she sighed.

"Marc, please go upstairs with Nana." Noelle set her hands on the boy's shoulders and turned him until he faced her. When he looked up and met her gaze, she gave him a reassuring smile. "I need to speak with this man."

This man. This *man*? Christian fumed. He was the boy's *father*.

"Are you sure, Mama?" Marc demanded, not backing down for a second.

"Absolutely." Noelle ruffled her son's dark hair, doing an excellent job of disguising her tension. "Please go upstairs. I'll come talk to you in a few minutes."

With a guard dog's sullen disapproval, the boy leveled a fierce glare at Christian before turning away. Despite the outrage battering him, pride rose in Christian. His son was brave and protective. Good traits for a future king.

Noelle waited until her son was shepherded upstairs by a woman in her midfifties before she stepped out of the house and pulled the door shut behind her. Noelle's eyes blazed, the heat of her annoyance radiating from her in the cool night air. "How dare you come here and say something like that in front of my son. *My* son."

"You've kept a pretty big secret from me all these years."

She shook her head at him. "You need to go."

"You're mistaken. I need answers."

"You will not get them tonight." With her mouth set in a determined line and her hands set on her hips, she let her gaze drill into him.

"Noelle, I'm sorry for what happened between us in the past." He let his voice settle into the cajoling tone that always made women give in. "I know you think what I did to you was insensitive, but I deserve to know my son."

"Deserve?" Her chest heaved with each agitated breath she took. "Deserve? Do you remember telling me five years ago that I should move on with my life and forget I ever met you?"

His heart twisted as he recalled that gut wrenching speech. "At the time I was right."

"I loved you."

"It wasn't going to work between us."

"It still isn't." She glared at him.

Her anger told him she still resented the way he'd dismissed her five years ago, but she'd come back to Sherdana to live her life. A life he'd told her he wanted no part of. And she'd been doing great without him.

Better than he'd done without her.

"Don't you see," he began, regret a heavy weight on his shoulders. "For everyone's sake, we're going to have to make peace. I intend to be a part of Marc's life."

"I'll not have you put my son through the same heart-ache I endured."

Her words were meant to wound, but Christian barely felt their sting. He was completely distracted by the vibrant beauty of the woman standing up to him. Never before had Noelle's temper flared like this. He regarded her in mesmerized fascination. When they'd been together before, she'd been so agreeable, so accommodating. The sex between them had always been explosive, but outside the bedroom she'd never demonstrated a hint of rebellion.

Now, she was a mother protecting her child. Her fierceness enthralled him. Abruptly the idea of reigniting their friendship seemed far too bland a proposition. He wanted her back in his bed. That she'd produced a potential heir to the throne made the whole situation clear-cut. He intended to marry her, and one day his son would be Sherdana's king.

"He's not just your son, Noelle. He's an Alessandro. Sherdanian royalty." Christian let the statement hang in the air between them for several beats. "Are you planning on keeping that from him?"

"Yes." But despite her forceful declaration, her expression told him she'd asked herself the same question. "No." Noelle stalked over to where his car sat in her driveway. "Damn you, Christian. He was never supposed to know."

"Then why did you bring him back here?" He followed her, repressing the urge to snatch her into his arms and see if she'd yield beneath his kisses the way she used to. "You could have very easily lived the rest of your life in France or gone to the United States." Had she come back to be close to him?

"My stepfather died two-and a-half years ago, leaving my mother alone. I came back to be near her."

His heart twisted at her explanation. Noelle's mother

had remarried when Noelle was six. "I'm sorry to hear that. I know you two were very close. You must miss him very much."

"I do." Sorrow tempered her irritation. "It's been a hard time for all of us. Marc loved his papi."

Regret assaulted Christian. Marc had another papi that he'd never know if Noelle got her way. That wasn't fair to any of them.

"Why didn't you lie and deny that he's mine."

She regarded him in bemusement. "Even if he didn't have the Alessandro features, why would I do that? Have I ever been untruthful with you?"

No. He'd been the one who'd held tight to secrets. "You kept my son from me for over four years."

"And if you'd made an attempt to contact me, I would have told you he existed."

"What about tonight? You weren't particularly forthcoming. If Marc hadn't come to the door, you'd never have admitted he existed."

"You aren't interested in being a father."

"That's not true." But in reality, he hadn't thought much about fatherhood other than as a duty demanded of him by his position.

"The whole country is buzzing about Sherdana's need for an heir, and they look to you as the country's last hope to produce one." Her somber tone matched his own dour meditations on the subject. She was no more convinced of his worthiness for the task than he was. "And now here's my son. Your heir. A simple solution to your problems."

A solution perhaps, but not necessarily a simple one. He had a duty to the throne and his country. It was up to him to secure the line of succession with a son. His burden had grown lighter with the revelation that he had a son, but his troubles were far from over.

"He can't be my heir," Christian said, his heart hammering as he regarded Noelle, curious to see if she'd connect the dots.

She'd always had a knack for discerning the true intent behind his actions. Except for the last time they'd been together five years earlier. He'd hidden his heart too well when he'd broken off their relationship.

When she remained silent, he continued. "Unless I marry his mother."

"Marry?" Her voice hitched.

He should try to convince her that that's why he'd come by tonight. Suddenly he knew this was the exact right thing to do. Marrying her would solve all his problems. Now that he'd seen her again, he realized there was no other woman in the world he could imagine being married to. Five years earlier they'd built a relationship on friendship and passion. He'd been a spoiled prince, and she'd been a naïve commoner who adored him. Instead of appreciating the gift of her love, he'd taken her for granted. He'd never understood why her generous spirit had brought out the worst in him. She'd loved him, flaws and all, and he'd been self-destructive and stupid. It made no sense, but he couldn't stop punishing her for loving him too much.

"You'd make a terrific princess," he said, and meant it. "The country already loves you."

"I made two wedding dresses. That's not enough to make me *worthy* of anyone's love." She shook her head. "You have aristocratic women from all over Europe eager to become your wife."

"But I don't want anyone else."

"Are you saying you want me?" She shook her head and laughed bitterly. "You want Marc." A pause. "You can't have him."

Christian could see there would be no convincing her

tonight, and he needed some time to assimilate all that he'd learned. He had a son. The impact had only begun to register.

"We will talk tomorrow," he said. "I will pick you up at noon. Clear your schedule for a few hours."

"I could clear my schedule for a few months and you'd get the same answer. I'm not going to give you my son."

"I don't want to take him from you." He hated that this was her perception of him, but he'd made her believe he was a villain so what else could he expect? "But I intend to be in his life."

Noelle stared at Christian, the urge to shriek building in her. She pressed her lips together as her mind raced. The cat was out of the bag. No way it was going back in. Christian knew he had a son.

*I don't want to take him from you.*

She pondered his words, hearing the warning. He wasn't foolish enough to tell her outright that he planned to take Marc away, but what Sherdanian court would let her keep her son if Prince Christian fought her for custody? For a second Noelle had a hard time breathing. Then she remembered an illegitimate son was no use to him. Christian needed her help to legitimize Marc's claim to the crown.

Her son a king.

Her knees bumped together at the thought. Marc was only four. It wasn't fair to upend his life in this way. She'd seen what being a royal had done to Christian. He'd grown up resentful and reckless. The third heir, he'd had all the privileges and none of the responsibility. She'd lost count of how many times he'd complained that he wished everyone would just leave him alone.

But with Crown Prince Gabriel and Princess Olivia unable to have children, and second-in-line Prince Nicolas married to an American, Marc wouldn't be a spare heir. He'd be in direct line to the throne.

"Noelle." Christian reclaimed her attention by touching her arm. "Don't make this hard on everyone."

Even through her thin sweater his warmth seeped into her skin. She jerked free before the heat invaded her muscles, rendering her susceptible to his persuasion. Her heart quickened as she backed out of range. It was humiliating how quickly her body betrayed her. A poignant reminder to keep her distance lest physical desire influence her decisions.

Five years ago she hadn't any reason to guard herself against him. She'd belonged to him heart, mind and soul. That was before he'd demonstrated how little she meant to him. It still hurt how easily he'd cast her aside.

Fierce determination heated her blood. Her cheeks grew hot. She'd do everything in her power to make sure he didn't do the same thing to Marc.

"You mean don't make it hard on you." Her tone bitter, she noted the way his eyes flickered, betraying his surprise.

Through all his past selfish behavior, she'd reminded herself that as a commoner of passing prettiness and limited sophistication she was lucky he'd sought her out at all. Pliable as a willow tree, she'd demonstrated patience and understanding. But having her heart broken had given her a spine, and five years of training in the cutthroat world of fashion design had forged that spine into tempered steel. If he continued to push her, he would discover what she was made of.

"But you're right," she added, deciding that arguing would only make him more determined to get his way. In addition, while she might no longer be a doormat, she hadn't lost touch with what was fair. "You are Marc's fa-

ther and deserve a chance to get to know him. Call me
at my office tomorrow at ten. I will check my schedule,
and we can figure out a time to meet and discuss a visitation schedule." Seeing Christian's dissatisfaction, Noelle
added, "You will do this my way, or I will take Marc beyond your reach."

Christian was used to getting his way in all things. The
way his eyebrows came together told Noelle she'd pushed
too far. But she held her gaze steady, letting him see her
stubbornness. In the end he nodded. From the glint in his
eyes, she doubted his acquiescence would last long. In
business he was known as a clever negotiator. She would
have to watch for his tricks.

Glancing up at the house, she spied a small figure sil-
houetted in an upstairs window. Marc's bedroom overlooked the front yard. He wasn't going to go to bed without
some sort of explanation from her. Sometimes he could
be wiser than a child twice his years. It was partially her
fault. She routinely gave him responsibilities, and Marc
knew there would be consequences if he didn't keep his
toys picked up, the garden watered and help shuffle his
clothes to and from the laundry.

"I have to get my son to bed," Noelle said. "I'll speak
with you tomorrow."

"Noelle." Christian spoke her name softly, halting her.
"I meant what I said earlier. I really do miss you. I'd like
for us to be friends again."

If he'd tried to cajole her regarding Marc, she might
have softened toward him. Christian had a right to his
son, whether she liked it or not, and his determination to
have a relationship with Marc would eventually soothe her
ferocious mama bear instincts. But the instant he tried to
appeal to what had once been between them, all sympa-
thy for him fled.

"I have a life filled with family, friends and purpose that I love. There's no room for you in it." She resumed walking toward the house without a backward glance. "Good night, Christian."

She didn't collapse after shutting the front door behind her, although she leaned back against the wood panel and breathed heavily for a few minutes until her heartbeat slowed. Had she really just faced down Christian and gotten the last word in? If her stomach wasn't pitching and rolling in reaction, she might have thrown a fist into the air.

Instead, Noelle headed upstairs. With each slow, deliberate step she regained the poise she'd learned in the stressful world of high fashion. The last thing she wanted was to upset her son and give him a reason to distrust Christian. Despite her measured pace, when she got to Marc's room, she still hadn't figured out a good way to explain the unexpected arrival of his father, a man she'd never talked about.

No surprise that Marc was jumping on his bed. On a regular day his small body contained enough energy to power a small village. After tonight's drama, he was a supernova.

"Mama. Mama. Mama."

"You know better than to jump on the bed," she scolded, stifling a heartfelt sigh. At least her mother had been able to get Marc into his pajamas. "Did you brush your teeth?" When her son showed no indication of answering her question, she glanced at her mother, who nodded. With deliberate firmness Noelle urged her son beneath the covers.

"Did you make the bad man go away?"

Time to correct her first mistake of the evening: letting Marc become aware of the tension between her and Christian.

"That wasn't a bad man, Marc. He was your prince."

Aversion twisted her son's features, amusing Noelle as she imagined the hit to Christian's ego at being so disparaged by one of his subjects.

"Don't like him."

Noelle wasn't feeling all that charitable toward Christian at the moment, either. She scooted her son into the middle of the double bed and seated herself beside him. Drawing in a breath, she braced herself to tell Marc that Christian was his father and then hesitated.

She couldn't bring herself to drop this bomb on her son until she figured out if having Christian in his life would benefit him. "Prince Christian would like to be your friend."

His little face screwed up in suspicion. "Does he like dinosaurs?"

"I don't know."

"Can he play football?"

"I'm not sure." Noelle suspected Marc had a list of activities he wanted to know about and smoothly redirected the conversation. "You'll have to ask him what he likes to do when you see him next."

"Will he get me a Komodo dragon?"

In addition to being obsessed with dinosaurs, Marc had a fascination with lizards and had received a twenty-gallon tank and a seven-inch leopard gecko from her dear friend Geoff for his fourth birthday. Since then, Marc had been lobbying for a bearded dragon, which would be twice the size of his current pet and require double the space.

"You know very well that a Komodo dragon is not a pet. They are seven feet long."

"But he could keep it at the palace, and I could visit it."

As wild a notion as this was, Noelle wouldn't put it past Christian to buy his son's love with a new pet. She would have to warn Christian against such a purchase.

The last thing she needed was a houseful of tanks containing lizards.

"That's not going to happen." She steered the conversation back on track. "Prince Christian might come to visit in the near future and if you have anything you want to know about that, I want you to ask me." She brushed a lock of hair off Marc's forehead and stared into his gold eyes. "Okay?"

The way her son was looking at her, Noelle suspected she'd bungled the conversation, but to her surprise she wasn't barraged by questions.

"Okay."

"Good. What do you want me to read tonight?"

Unsurprisingly he picked up a book on dinosaurs. Marc enjoyed looking at the pictures as she read the descriptions. Noelle knew he had the entire volume memorized. The cover was worn, and a few of the pages had minor tears. Her active son was hard on most things, and this book was one of his favorites.

It took half an hour to get through the book. Marc had forgotten all about Christian's visit by the time Noelle reached the last page. To her relief he settled down without a fight, his head on the pillow. A glance at the clock told her it was not long past his normal bedtime, and she congratulated herself on her minor victory.

Downstairs, her mother had opened a bottle of her favorite Gavi, a crisp Italian white with delicate notes of apples and honey. She handed Noelle a glass without asking if she wanted any.

"I thought you might be in the mood to celebrate," Mara said, eyeing her daughter over the rim of her glass.

Resentment burned at her mother's passive-aggressive remark. "Because Christian discovered I've been hiding his son all these years?" She snorted. "For the thousandth time, I'm not in love with him."

Mara didn't argue. "What are his intentions toward Marc?"

"He wants to get to know him."

"And that's all?"

"Of course. What else could there be?" Noelle had gone outside and shut the door before her conversation with Christian had gone too far, and knew her mother hadn't overheard anything. Still, she experienced a flash of despair as she recalled how Christian had raised the notion of legitimizing Marc by marrying her.

"The kingdom needs an heir. Now that both Prince Gabriel and Prince Nicolas are married, the media are obsessively speculating who your Prince Christian will choose to marry. The pressure is all on him to produce a son."

"He's not my Prince Christian," Noelle muttered, letting her irritation show.

"And now he knows he has a son."

"An illegitimate son." Noelle wanted to take back the reminder as soon as her mother's eyes lit with malicious delight.

"And here you are single and Sherdanian. Not to mention still harboring unrequited feelings for him."

"Don't be ridiculous. I'm not going to marry Christian so that he can claim Marc as his heir."

Her mother didn't look convinced. "Wouldn't it be your dream come true?"

"You were living in Italy when I met Christian, so you don't know what it was like between us. He's not husband material, and I'm not going to marry him because he needs an heir." Noelle heard heartbreak beneath the fervor in her voice. Five years had passed, but she hadn't fully recovered from the hurt dealt to her when Christian pushed her out of his life.

It wasn't something she intended to forgive or forget.

The café table on his cramped, third-floor balcony was big enough for a cup of coffee and a small pot of hot pink petunias. Christian sat on one of the two chairs, ignoring the laptop balanced on his knee while he stared down the narrow street whose details were lost to shadow at this early hour. Thoughts on the encounter with Noelle the night before, he watched the light seep into this old section of Sherdana's capital city of Carone.

Although Christian had rooms in the palace for his use, he rarely stayed there, preferring the privacy of his own space. He'd lost track of how many homes he owned. He did business all over Europe and had apartments in the major cities where he spent the most time. He owned two homes in Sherdana: this cozy two-bedroom apartment in the center of the capital where he could walk to bakeries, cafés and restaurants, and a castle on a premier vineyard two hours north of Carone.

After discovering he was a father, Christian had lain in bed, staring at the ceiling while his thoughts churned. Eventually he'd decided to give up on sleep and catch up on his emails. Nic and Brooke had gotten married on a Wednesday, which meant Christian had lost an entire day of work. He usually worked from home until late morning. His active social life kept him out late most evenings, and if he saw the sun come up, it was more likely that he was coming home after a long night rather than getting an early start on the day.

Despite his good intentions, he couldn't concentrate on the reports that had been compiled by his CFO regarding his purchase of a small Italian company that was developing intelligent robot technology. The columns of numbers blurred and ran together as his mind refused to focus.

Noelle had borne him a son and hidden the truth for five years, a pretty amazing feat in this age of social media. Last night, as he'd driven back to the apartment, he'd been furious with her. It shouldn't have mattered that he'd let her believe he wanted their relationship to end. She'd been pregnant with his child. She should have told him. And then what? He'd thought letting her go to pursue her dream of being a designer in Paris had been the best thing for her. What would he have done if he'd known she was pregnant? Marry her?

Christian shook his head.

It wouldn't have crossed his mind. She'd known him well. Better than he'd known himself. As the third son, he'd had little responsibility to the monarchy and could do what he wanted. So he'd partied to excess, made a name for himself as a playboy, indulged his every desire and thought no further than the moment.

The accident had changed all that. Changed him. He'd risked his life to save someone and had been permanently scarred in the process. But the fire that had ravaged his right side had wrought other changes. His selfless actions had impaired his hedonistic proclivities. Made him aware of others' needs. Before the accident he'd enjoyed being selfish and irresponsible. Losing the ability to act without recognizing the consequences to others had been almost as painful as the slow mending of his burns.

Thus, when he arranged for Noelle to train in Paris, he'd known that letting her think he no longer wanted her in his life would break her heart. Hurting her had pained him more than sending her away, but he'd known that if she stayed with him, he risked doing her far greater harm.

And now, thanks to his discovery of their son, she was back in his life. He ached with joy and dread.

Showing up on her doorstep last night had been a return to old patterns. When they'd been together before, he'd often popped by unannounced late at night after the clubs closed.

He'd met her at the café near his apartment where she waitressed. Unlike most of the women he flirted with, she hadn't been intrigued by his title or swayed by his charm. She'd treated him with such determined professionalism that he'd been compelled to pursue her relentlessly until she agreed to see him outside of work.

They didn't date. Not in a traditional sense. She was too serious to enjoy his frivolous lifestyle and too sensible to fit in with his superficial friends. But she was exactly what he needed. Her apartment became his refuge. When they finally became lovers, after being friends for six months, she was more familiar to him than any woman he'd ever known.

Not that this had stopped him from taking her for granted, first as a friend and confidante, and then as the woman who came alive in his arms.

Christian closed his eyes and settled his head back against the brick facade of his apartment. The breath he blew out didn't ease the tightness in his chest or relax the clenched muscles of his abdomen.

Last night he'd suggested that they should marry. The ease with which the words had slipped off his tongue betrayed the fact that his subconscious was already plotting. Speaking with her at the party had obviously started something brewing. Why not marry Noelle? The notion made sense even before he'd found out about Marc.

Years before they'd been good together. Or at least she'd been good for him. Sexually they'd been more than compatible. She'd been a drug in his system. One he'd tried numerous times to purge with no luck.

Discovering they'd created a child together, a much-needed potential heir to the throne, pretty much cemented his decision to make her his princess. He didn't need to scour Europe trying to find his future wife. She was right under his nose.

He should have felt as if an enormous weight had been lifted from his shoulders, but long ago he'd developed a conscience where Noelle was concerned. After the way he'd broken things off five years ago, she didn't want him anywhere near her. Persuading her to marry him would take time, and once the media got wind of his interest, they would interfere at every turn.

He'd have to work fast. She'd loved him once. A few intimate dinners to remind her of their crazy-hot chemistry and she'd be putty in his hands. Christian shoved aside a twinge of guilt. Being cavalier about seducing Noelle was not in keeping with the man he'd become these past few years. Scheming was something he reserved for business dealings.

Christian headed inside to shower and get dressed. For his country and his family, he had to convince Noelle to marry him. If it benefited him in the process, so much the better.

# Three

An extravagant arrangement of two dozen long-stemmed red roses awaited Noelle in her office at the back of her small dress shop in Sherdana's historic city center. Coffee in hand, she stopped dead just inside the door and sucked in the rich, sweet scent of the enormous blossoms. She plucked a small white envelope from the bouquet, but didn't need to read the card to know the sender. The scarlet blooms signaled Christian's intent to stir up her quiet, perfectly ordered world.

Knowing she would get nothing accomplished with the roses dominating her efficient gold-and-cream space, Noelle called her assistant.

"Please get these out of here." Noelle waved her hand dismissively. When curiosity lit Jeanne's eyes, Noelle realized she'd let her irritation show.

Jeanne scooped the vase off the low coffee table. "Should I put them in the reception room?"

Noelle wanted to tell Jeanne to drop them into the trash out back. "Why don't you put them in the workroom? That way the seamstresses could enjoy the flowers."

"Are you sure you don't want me to leave them here? They're so beautiful."

Noelle's temper flared, sharp and acidic. Lack of sleep and frayed nerves were to blame for her reaction. She shook her head and strove to keep her voice calm as she tried to put a positive spin on her request. "Everyone has been working so hard. The flowers are for all of us," she lied, feeling only the mildest twinge of guilt at deceiving her employee.

Once the flowers were gone, Noelle opened her office window to the beautiful morning and let in the fresh air, but after an hour she could swear the scent of the roses remained. Restless and edgy, Noelle slid her sketchbook into her briefcase. She would go to her favorite café and work on the designs for next winter's collection.

The bell on the front door jangled, announcing a visitor. Because of her location among the quaint shops in the historic district, occasionally someone passing by would pop in, stirred by curiosity. Noelle's shop carried no ready to wear wedding dresses, but because her wealthy clientele could often be difficult to please, she had several bridal gowns on hand that had been rejected for one reason or another.

Jeanne's greeting carried down the hall as she approached whoever had entered the shop. Noelle gathered several pencils and froze in the act of dropping them into her briefcase. A deep voice rumbled in response to her assistant's inquiring tone. The pencils clattered as they fell from Noelle's nerveless fingers. Strong footsteps rang on the wood floor of the narrow hallway leading to her office.

Feeling much like a cornered cat, Noelle glanced up and saw Christian's imposing shoulders filling the doorway.

Cross that he'd followed up the flower delivery with a personal appearance, she spoke with unusual bluntness. "You were supposed to call me at ten not show up unannounced."

"I came to see if you liked the roses." He took in her pristine office and frowned. "Didn't you receive them?"

"Yes. I put them in the workroom for my employees to enjoy."

Not one muscle twitched in his face to betray his reaction, but she could tell her answer displeased him. She hated the way guilt rushed through her.

"I sent them to you."

All the time they'd been together, he'd never once given her flowers. She'd understood her role in his life. First as a sounding board for all his frustrations and woes. Eventually, she'd become his lover, a convenient one that he could drop in on whenever he was feeling lonely or in need of comfort. She'd made no demands, expected nothing, and he'd given her mind-blowing sex in return. To be fair, while they'd been physically intimate she'd also enjoyed a great deal of emotional intimacy, as well. But out of bed, Christian donned the charming persona he maintained to keep people at bay.

The roses had reminded her how susceptible she'd once been to his charm. What if nothing had changed in the past five years? She needed to determine if she could trust her head to guide her. He mustn't be allowed to think he could sway her with romantic gestures. For gestures were all they were.

"You're not going to make this easy for me, are you?" He crossed the threshold, crowding her office with his powerful presence.

"Why should I?" Noelle liked having her elegant desk as a buffer between them, but didn't want her entire staff hearing this conversation. Stepping out from behind the desk, she gestured Christian away from the door and closed it, trapping them together in the small space. "Five years ago you wanted nothing more to do with me. Now, you're desperate for an heir and you want my son."

"You forget that I came to see you last night knowing nothing about Marc," he grumbled in his deep, beguiling voice. His intent was clear. He intended to throw every trick in his abundant arsenal at her. "I saw you at the wedding and knew I'd made a mistake letting you go all those years ago."

His claim was so ridiculous she should have laughed in his face. But the words made her chest ache. How many nights had she lain awake, praying for his knock on her apartment door in Paris? Dreaming that he'd burst in, sweep her off her feet and declare he'd been a fool to let her go and that he couldn't live without her. Too many. In fact, she hadn't given up all hope until Marc's first birthday.

"I don't believe you."

"If you give me a chance, I'll prove it to you." His dark gold eyes glittered with sensual intent.

A hysterical laugh bubbled up in her chest. She clamped her teeth together and fought to appear unflustered. No easy task when the masculine scent of the man awakened buried memories. A tingle began between her thighs as she relived the joy of his hands on her body, his lips on hers.

Last night she'd stood up to him, an alarmed mama bear protecting her cub. Today she was a woman confronting a man who intended to persuade and seduce. Heat bloomed in her cheeks. She scowled, angry with herself and taking it out on him.

"If you want me to take your interest in Marc seriously,

you'd be better off demonstrating that you have what it takes to be a father."

"I agree." He nodded. "Which is why I sent a gift to Marc, as well."

Noelle bit back a groan. "What sort of gift?"

"A small thing."

"How small?"

"A child-sized electric car. My assistant said her son loves to drive his cousin's. He is about Marc's age."

She hissed out a breath. "You can't just do that."

"Of course I can."

Once upon a time she'd have teased him about his arrogance. Once upon a time she'd been madly in love with him.

"An electric car is an expensive toy. I want Marc to value art and stories and music. Not things."

"He's a four-year-old boy," Christian scoffed. "They want to get muddy and have adventures."

Noelle knew it was ridiculous, but she could feel Marc slipping away from her with each word Christian spoke. Her son would love this thrill-seeking prince and want to go live in a palace, and never once miss his mother. "And you're an expert on four-year-old boys?"

"I was one once. And he's a prince. He should always get the best."

Panic rose. Her voice dropped to a whisper. "That's not how I'm raising him."

"We need to be together for Marc's sake." Christian caught her hand and gave it a gentle squeeze. "He shouldn't have to grow up without a father."

Christian seemed sincere enough, but Noelle couldn't ignore that he needed an heir and knew just how stubborn Christian could be when he wanted something. She tugged her hand free and squared her shoulders.

"I can't possibly be with you," she said. "I'm involved with someone and we're quite serious."

Christian absorbed Noelle's statement with a slow eye-blink, his thoughts reeling. He'd come in too confident, certain that he could win over Noelle with a few roses and a bit of persuasion. She'd always been there any time he needed her. It had never once occurred to him that she might be in love with someone else. Acid burned in his gut at the thought of her with anyone besides him.

"You didn't mention anyone last night."

Her expression, once so transparent and open, betrayed none of her thoughts. "All I thought about was Marc and the effect your sudden appearance in his life would have on him."

"Who is this man you're seeing?" The question sounded more like an interrogation than a friendly inquiry.

"Someone I met shortly after I moved to Paris."

Five years. Had she run into his arms after Christian had sent her away? A knot formed in his chest.

"I'd love to meet him. Does he live in Sherdana?"

"Ah." Suddenly she looked very uncertain. "No. He splits his time between Paris and London."

Christian was liking this more and more. "Long distance affairs are so difficult," he purred. "As I'm sure you're finding out."

"Geoff loves Marc."

Christian saw resolve blazing in the depths of her chestnut-colored eyes.

"And Marc loves Geoff. They have a great time together. *We* are good together."

He wondered at her vehemence. Was she trying to convince him that this Geoff character was father material or convince herself that he was husband material? Either way,

Christian saw a foothold that would allow him to breach her defenses.

"When does he plan to come to Sherdana next?" A long unused oubliette beneath the castle on Christian's vineyard might be the perfect place to stash Geoff until Noelle came to her senses.

"Why?" Noelle regarded him with narrowed eyes.

"I'd like to meet him. Does he visit regularly?"

"Of course." But she didn't sound all that sure of her answer. "That is, when his cases permit. He's the managing partner of a very successful law firm specializing in human rights law and extradition." Pride softened her lips into a fond smile. "And of course, Marc and I travel to London and Paris quite often to visit him."

"How serious are you?" The more Christian heard, the less concerned he became that Geoff was going to prove a hindrance. If something of a permanent nature was going to happen between Noelle and her absent suitor, it should have occurred in the past five years. "Do you plan on marrying?"

She glanced down at her clasped hands. "We've discussed the possibility, but haven't made anything official."

What sort of man waited five years to claim a woman like Noelle? A very stupid one. And that was just fine with him. Christian had no qualms about stealing Noelle out from beneath the man's nose.

"Have dinner with me tonight."

Her eyes widened at his abrupt invitation, but she shook her head. "I can't. Geoff—"

"Isn't here and from the sound of things isn't likely to visit any time soon." A half step brought him close enough to hear her sharp intake of breath and feel the way her muscles tensed as he traced his knuckles along her jawline. The old, familiar chemistry sparked between them.

"You deserve a man who will appreciate you every minute of every day, not whenever his business dealings permit."

Noelle batted his hand away. "What would you know about how I deserve to be appreciated? When we were together, the only time you concerned yourself about my needs was when we were in bed."

"You make it sound like that's a bad thing." He spoke lightly, hiding his regret that he'd hurt her. He'd been a selfish bastard when they were together and hadn't grasped her worth. How ironic that finally understanding her value had compelled him to send her away.

Yet was he behaving any less selfishly now? After ignoring her for five years, he'd suddenly decided to drag her back into his life because he needed her once again. Was it fair to disrupt the tranquil, comfortable world she'd made for herself? Probably not, but now that he'd begun, Christian couldn't bring himself to stop. They'd made a child together. He had a son. That wasn't something he intended to walk away from.

"Christian, you weren't good for me five years ago, and you're not going to be good for me now. I was so madly in love with you I was happy with whatever scraps of your life you were willing to share with me. That's not enough for me anymore. I have a son who deserves to be loved and nurtured. He is my primary focus. Every decision I make is with his best interests foremost in my mind."

Christian's temper flared. "And you don't think his mother being married to his father is the best thing for him?"

"Not if the only reason his parents marry is so the Alessandro line continues to rule Sherdana."

Christian wasn't accustomed to cynicism coming from Noelle. She'd been sweet, innocent and as trusting as a kitten. His opposite in every way. It was why he hadn't been able to give her up even when he started to see shadows darken her eyes and her smiles become forced.

"Making Marc my heir is not the only reason I want to marry you." Although it was an important one to be sure. "I can't forget how good we were together."

Noelle shook her head. "I'm not sure you were good for me."

"I'm no longer the man I was." In so many ways that was true. He'd lost the ability to be frivolous and irresponsible. "The accident saw to that."

She flinched. "And I'm not the woman you once knew. Who's to say it would even work between us anymore?"

"Who's to say it wouldn't be better?"

As if to demonstrate his point, Christian slid his fingers around the back of her neck and drew her toward him. Without giving her a second to process his action, he lowered his lips to her and drank in her sweetness. A groan gathered in his chest at the way her mouth yielded to him. She gasped softly as her lips parted. He remembered all the times he'd held her in his arms and indulged his need for her with long, drugging kisses.

With other women he'd been quick to get to his pleasure. He liked his lovemaking hot and frenzied. Being with Noelle had brought out a different side of his personality. He'd never been in a rush with her. Her warm, silken skin and the gentle rise and fall of her slender curves had been worth appreciating in great detail. He'd adored her every gasp and shiver as he learned what pleased her. After a month he knew her body better than any woman he'd ever been with and yet she continued to surprise him.

Desire buzzed in his veins, the intensity rising as Noelle leaned into him. He freed her lips before longing made the kiss spiral out of control. Heart thumping madly, he inhaled her light floral perfume. The fragrance was more sophisticated than what she used to wear, reminding him that time and distance had made them strangers. His lids felt heavy as he lifted his lashes and regarded her flushed cheeks.

"You didn't stop me from kissing you," he murmured in satisfaction, wondering if it could really be this easy.

"I was curious how it would feel after five long years." Her neutral tone dampened his optimism.

"And?"

"Your technique hasn't diminished."

Christian stepped back and gave her a lopsided smile. "Nor has my desire for you."

"Yes...well." She didn't sound as if she believed him. "I'm sure you can find any number of women eager to distract you."

"It's not like that anymore."

"The tabloids say otherwise."

"The tabloids exaggerate. Any drama attributed to my love life is concocted to sell newspapers."

"So how do you explain the twin models from Milan photographed topless on your hotel balcony in Cannes?"

"They needed a place to crash and I spent the night on the phone to Hong Kong."

Noelle's lips thinned as she nodded. "And the Spanish heiress who ran away from her wedding with you?"

"It was an arranged marriage and she was in love with an architect from Brussels who happened to be doing some work on my apartment in London."

"You're asking me to believe you're in the habit of rescuing women these days?"

He understood her skepticism. Five years earlier his playboy reputation had been well earned. But the day he'd arranged for Noelle to study in Paris was the day he'd begun to change. She'd been the first woman he'd saved. And the only one who'd needed to be rescued from him.

"There's a long list of women I've helped. I could put you in touch with some of them if it would help improve your perception of me." She wasn't going to take his pursuit seriously if she thought he hadn't changed.

"I'm sure there are scads of women who would line up to sing your praises."

"Have dinner with me." He repeated his earlier invitation, determined to convince her this wasn't a ploy or a scam. "We have a great deal to talk about."

She shook her head. "The only thing that concerns me is your intentions for my son. We can talk about ground rules here or at your office. There's no reason for us to become more than civil acquaintances."

"That's where you're wrong. I can name several very good reasons why we should take our relationship to a close, personal level. Starting with the fact that I make you nervous." He caught her chin and turned her face so he could snare her gaze. "I think that means you still have feelings for me. I know I have feelings for you. We belong together."

"I'm with Geoff. Nothing you can say or do will change that."

Christian slid his thumb across her lower lip and watched her pupils dilate. No doubt she was counting on her words and actions to effectively put him off, but there was no hiding her body's reaction.

With a slow smile, his hand fell away. "We'll see."

# Four

With her pulse hammering in her ears, Noelle spent a full minute staring at the empty hallway after Christian had gone. What had just happened? Knees shaking, she retreated to her desk and dropped into her comfortable chair with a hearty exhalation. To her dismay, her fingers trembled as she dialed a familiar number. When Geoff answered the phone, his deep voice acted like a sturdy net she could fall into and be safe.

"Geoff, thank goodness."

"Noelle, are you okay? You sound upset."

"I've just done a terrible, cowardly thing." Such drama wasn't like her, and she noticed that several beats passed while Geoff adjusted to her tumultuous state.

"I'm sure it's not as bad as all that."

She closed her eyes, and his steady tone calmed her. She'd met Geoff shortly after moving to Paris. He'd been at a party her boss was throwing and they'd hit it off immediately. Both had been grieving losses. Noelle was fresh from her breakup with Christian and Geoff had lost his wife of fifteen years to cancer six months earlier.

"It's really bad. I made up a serious relationship between you and me."

Amusement filled his voice as he asked, "Couldn't you just have told the guy you weren't interested? That's worked for you up to this point."

Normally Noelle blamed her lack of interest in men on the demands of her skyrocketing career and being focused on her son. The truth was she didn't find anyone as interesting or attractive as Christian. In the darkest hours of the night when she couldn't sleep and got up to sketch or visit her workshop, she suspected that the love she'd thought had died when Christian cast her aside was really only buried beneath a thick layer of pain and disappointment.

"It's not just a guy." In her agitation, she snapped one of her drawing pencils in two. "It's Christian, and he figured out Marc is his son."

"Ah." Geoff had been a shoulder to cry on when she'd first discovered she was pregnant. Seventeen years her senior, he'd been a combination of close friend and elder brother.

"I told you about the delicate political situation surrounding the Sherdanian throne. Yesterday Nicolas Alessandro married an American girl, leaving Christian the only brother capable of producing a future king. Last night he came to the house and met Marc. Now he's got it in his head that we should get married so Marc can be his legitimate heir."

"And he won't take no for an answer?"

"He's determined to win me over." Noelle trembled as her mind replayed the kiss. She hadn't forgotten the chemistry between them, but five years had dulled her memory of how susceptible she was to his touch. "I can't let that happen."

"So you told him we were dating?"

"I panicked. Which was stupid because he doesn't believe me. I need to show him that you exist and that we're very happy. Can you come spend the weekend with me? I'll call and invite him to have dinner with us." Silence greeted her announcement. "Geoff? I'm sorry, I know I'm putting you on the spot."

"Noelle, darling, you know I'm happy to help you any way I can, but are you sure this is the best tactic? I don't live in Sherdana. Even if I appear once and we give a great performance of being madly in love, he's not going to be dissuaded by an absent lover."

She thought back to Christian's remark about long distance relationships. "You're right. Call Jean-Pierre and ask him if I can borrow an engagement ring. A big one." The jeweler owed her several favors for sending business his way.

"Our relationship is moving awfully fast," Geoff teased, but concern shaded his lighthearted tone.

"I know and I'm sorry. I'm taking terrible advantage of our friendship, but I'm feeling rather desperate at the moment."

"There's no one I'd be happier to be fake-engaged to than you, but have you thought this through? Are you planning on staying engaged forever? What happens when we don't actually get married?"

"Hopefully he will be under enough pressure to marry someone suitable that he'll realize he can't wait around to change my mind."

"This plan of yours is full of holes."

Christian had a knack for shredding her customarily

sensible behavior. "We can talk about that when you get here."

"Very well. I'll see you Friday evening."

Noelle disconnected the call feeling marginally less anxious. Pretending to be engaged to Geoff was a ridiculous ploy, but hopefully one that would buy her enough space to get her emotions back under control. Christian had been on the offensive since Brooke and Nic's wedding. Every step he'd taken had backed Noelle into a corner. It was time she came out swinging.

Christian sat at his favorite table in Seillan's, one of Carone's finest restaurants featuring French cuisine. It was owned by a long-time friend of his, world-renowned chef Michel Seillan.

"Hello, P.C. Are you dining alone?" Michel gripped Christian's shoulder in an affectionate vise. The two men had gone to school together since they were seven years old and had spent a great deal of time tearing up the clubs of London and Paris in their early twenties. The nickname P.C. had evolved when Michel had complained that addressing Christian as Prince Christian took too long.

"No, I'm expecting a couple of friends."

"Female? And are you needing some help to entertain them?"

"Only one is a woman, and when have I ever needed help keeping women entertained?"

"Years ago, I might have agreed with you, but lately you've slowed down." Michel smirked.

"These days I'm more interested in quality than quantity."

With a laugh and another thump on Christian's shoulder, Michel departed. Minutes later a waiter appeared with a dry vodka martini. Christian resisted the urge to down the drink. For some reason, he wasn't feeling calm as the top of the hour approached.

Noelle might not be in love with the British barrister she was bringing to dinner, but that didn't mean the reverse was true. During the years when Christian and Noelle had been together, he'd never worried that another man might steal her away. She'd been devoted to him first as a friend and then as a lover. But that was before he'd sent her away. Before she'd had to raise their child on her own for four years.

Christian had never been one for settling down. No doubt Noelle continued to view him that way. The fact that he had to marry in order to produce an heir for the kingdom didn't exactly recommend his willingness or ability to be a good husband.

What if Noelle was ready to build a life with someone steady? To have more children? She'd want a man with a constant heart who'd devote unwavering attention to her needs.

The sip of the martini he'd taken stuck in Christian's suddenly tight throat. He coughed and coughed again as the liquor burned. Through watering eyes, he spotted Noelle entering the restaurant.

She was eye-catching in a fifties-inspired black dress with a bodice embroidered in gold flowers that hugged her torso and bared her arms. A wide band of black fabric made her waist look incredibly tiny, and the full skirt skimmed her knees. She wove between the tables with effortless grace, and Christian's heart twisted. The lively smile curving her full red lips was for the man who trailed after her. She'd always been pretty, but confidence and happiness had transformed her into a vivacious beauty. Desire stirred in Christian. But it wasn't his hormones that came to life. He wanted her, not just as a sexual partner, but as a supportive companion who lightened his bad moods and made his troubles fade away.

He'd forgotten how easily she aroused his emotions. How she made him ache for her laughter and long for the soothing caress of her fingers through his hair.

Christian stood as Noelle and her escort approached the table. The man was considerably older than Christian expected. Tall and lean, with blond hair and laugh lines around his gray eyes, he had close to two decades on Noelle. Seeing the level of fondness in her eyes, Christian was prepared to dislike the man intensely.

"Good evening, Noelle," Christian said, keeping his roiling emotions out of his tone.

"Good evening, Your Royal Highness. I would like to introduce you to Geoff Coomb. Geoff, this is Prince Christian Alessandro."

Noelle's companion had a firm handshake and returned Christian's assessing gaze with confidence that made Christian despise him even more. "It was kind of you to join us for dinner."

"Not at all."

*Us.*

The word on the man's lips bothered Christian more than he liked. It spoke of a familiarity that he no longer enjoyed with Noelle. He'd underestimated the threat her relationship with Coomb represented. While Christian had fully intended to convince Noelle to marry him through whatever means necessary, he'd presumed his methods would involve seduction and winning his son's love. He hadn't considered she might be perfectly happy with the affection and emotional support she received from Coomb.

Resisting the desire to scowl at the lawyer, Christian fixed a pleasant expression on his face and stepped forward to hold Noelle's chair out for her. To his annoyance,

Geoff was there a beat faster, and she flashed him another of her enchanting smiles as she sat. Christian waited until Coomb settled and then fell into the role of perfect host, all the while digging into the history between the two so he could figure out the best way to win Noelle back.

"Noelle told me you two met years ago in Paris."

"At a party," Geoff said, regarding Noelle with an intimate smile. "She was the most beautiful woman in the room."

Christian had little doubt of that. "And you've been together all these years?"

"We were friends awhile before we began to date," Noelle said, favoring Coomb with another of her glowing smiles. "Neither one of us was ready to jump into anything right away."

"I'd lost my wife a few months earlier to cancer." Geoff covered Noelle's right hand with his. "Noelle was a good friend to me. We grew very close."

Close was what Noelle and Christian had been until he'd ruined everything.

"Geoff kept me from quitting during that first year in Paris. Without his encouragement I would have run home at least once a week."

Despite the jealousy raging through him, Christian was glad Noelle had had someone to support her when he couldn't. He'd been too self-absorbed to appreciate what he had until it was too late. And then too stubborn to reach out and fix what he'd broken. After the accident, he'd reasoned Noelle had been better off without him. And he'd been right. She'd sacrificed too much to be with him.

But that was then. The noble part of him that had let her go five years earlier was no longer in charge of his actions. He was older and wiser these days. They had a son. She and Marc belonged with him.

The waiter brought Noelle a glass of red wine and a scotch for Coomb. As Noelle lifted her left hand to pick up her drink, the light from the chandelier overhead caught in the enormous diamond adorning her ring finger. Noelle noticed Christian's riveted attention, and her expression grew positively radiant.

"We're engaged."

"That's rather sudden." And convenient. The engagement had moved her beyond his grasp. Suspicious, Christian eyed the older man, hoping for some sign of subterfuge, but saw only fondness as the lawyer gazed at Noelle.

"Not sudden at all," Coomb replied. "We've been heading this way for years."

"You seemed content with the relationship as it was," Christian pointed out to Noelle. Had she been surprised by this turn of events, or was she guilty of deliberately misleading him? The Noelle he'd known had been free of guile. He didn't like to think she'd changed so much.

"I am content with our relationship in all its forms." Noelle gave Coomb a sweet smile. "I feel so very lucky to have such a wonderful man in my life."

Christian's gut ached as if he'd been kicked. Something ugly and dark formed inside him as he watched Noelle bask in Coomb's affection. Curses reverberated in Christian's thoughts. Being the uncomfortable third wheel wasn't how he'd expected the evening to go.

"But," she continued, fixing bright eyes on Christian. "I'm thrilled that we are going to be a family."

Was there a touch too much defiance in her delivery? Christian assessed her for a long moment before extending his arm to signal the attentive waiter. "We're celebrating," he told Antonio. "A bottle of champagne to toast the newly betrothed."

Inwardly seething, Christian waited while crystal flutes

were placed upon the table and filled, and then gave the newly engaged couple his most political smile. "May you enjoy a lifetime of happiness." She would assume that he meant her and Coomb.

Christian set the glass to his lips and drank the excellent vintage with little pleasure. While a part of him clamored to be the one she chose, more than anything he hoped she would be happy. *Idiot.* Why couldn't he stop doing the right thing where she was concerned? In all other aspects of his life he was a selfish bastard, but when it came to Noelle, he wanted what was best for her.

Of course, the solution was simple. He just needed to believe that the best thing for Noelle was for her to marry him.

In the days since he'd spoken to her at the latest royal wedding and discovered he was a father, Christian had lost numerous hours in daydreaming about his future with Noelle and Marc. Imagining long passion-filled nights in bed with her left him grinning in anticipation.

In contrast the thought of being a father distressed him. Nothing he'd done in his life had prepared him for such a daunting task. What part of buying troubled companies to tear apart and restructure gave him the skills to win the trust and affection of a four-year-old boy?

As a prince, he'd never had to work at making people like him. Those who didn't enjoy his company respected him because of his position. Foolish or ambitious women, who appreciated his money and position, vied for his attention. Sensible ones and those unsuitable for romancing he charmed without effort, but invested little of himself in the exchanges. His days and nights were consistently filled with an endless supply of business associates, social acquaintances or potential lovers. He cared little about any of them and his encounters blurred together in an indistinct gabble of memories.

Nothing about this shallow, drifting existence had bothered him until Noelle entered his life. She was a magnifying glass that sharpened his perceptions, making him see things as they were instead of as fuzzy renderings on the edges of his awareness. She'd provoked him to question why with all the money he made he wasn't using some of it to make a positive social impact. But when he'd donated to charities, he'd picked ones that would eventually provide a benefit to him and hadn't enjoyed the accolades heaped upon him.

Without meaning to she'd pushed him to do better. Be better. She'd never criticized his actions or made suggestions of things he should do, but as he discovered what was important to her, he'd begun to change. All his life he'd barely taken responsibility for himself, much less taken on the burden of anyone else's welfare. Suddenly he had this insignificant woman in his head all the time. In the morning he'd woken and wondered if she'd missed him in her bed. Throughout his day he noted things he wanted to share with her. She took up space in his narcissistic reality, and he resented her intrusion.

Realizing her effect on him had set off a chain reaction of bad behavior. She'd always forgive and forget, but that hadn't been the end of it for him.

He'd felt guilty.

And hated it.

Which had naturally led to even worse behavior and eventually the accident. Five years after the fact, that awful night continued to haunt him. He relived the pain and terror every time he caught a glimpse of his reflection or touched the puckered scars that marred his right arm and the right side of his chest, neck and face. The skin tingled in phantom pain. He could have undergone reconstructive surgery for the damage, but preferred to leave the scars as a reminder of his supreme failure.

Christian shook himself out of his dark thoughts and caught Noelle watching him. Worry, longing and regret raced across her face in rapid succession before she looked away. Christian stared at her as she laughed at something Coomb said to her. Was it possible that she still cared and was fighting desperately not to? Something inside Christian clicked into place like the resetting of a dislocated bone. He hadn't realized how out of whack his psyche had been until the pain vanished. In the peaceful aftermath, he began to plot.

Noelle might be engaged, but she wasn't married. The ring she wore represented a promise to wed, and he was notorious for making even the most stubborn, committed individuals change their minds.

Heart thumping in wild abandonment, Noelle gulped down the beginnings of panic. Despite the heartache and the half decade of separation, Christian continued to fascinate and disturb her like no other man. He'd been back in her life for three days, and her judgment was already lousy. She'd invented a fake fiancé and convinced Geoff to play along. All the while she fought against the longing to rake her fingers through Christian's thick, wavy hair and pull his mouth to hers.

Nothing good would come of getting caught up in the reckless desire that had hampered her innate common sense during the two years she'd loved him. He'd driven her to the highest peaks of ecstasy one day and left her wallowing in uncertainty and disappointment the next. Even accepting that she was responsible for her own happiness,

Noelle hadn't once barred her door or her heart against him. And in the end, he'd been the one to walk away.

Which was why she needed to be so careful now. There was more at stake than her foolish heart. She couldn't risk that Christian might hurt her son.

His son.

Noelle lifted her fork and held it suspended over the plate the waiter had placed before her. Her thoughts were too complex to sort out the ingredients of the elegantly plated meal. She saw her dinner as a mass of color: shades of brown from caramel to espresso, a range of greens and a golden sauce.

"Something wrong?" Christian prompted, his deep voice silky and sensual.

She made the mistake of meeting his burnished gold eyes. He looked as if he wanted to devour her right then and there. "It's too beautiful to eat."

His slow smile curled her toes. "I assure you it will taste even better."

Breathless in reaction to his dizzying charisma, Noelle jerked her attention back to the meal and admonished herself for letting him get to her. The cuisine that should have dazzled her palate tasted like sawdust in her dry mouth. When would Christian stop dominating her senses? She would have thought five years apart had dulled her body's reaction to him.

At least she maintained some control over her mind.

It probably helped that she had very little trouble resisting *Prince* Christian. Arrogant and confident, the royal persona represented everything that had broken her heart five years earlier. Especially when he'd shown up unannounced at her farmhouse after Nic and Brooke's wedding and presumed she'd marry him to legitimize Marc.

She gave her head a barely perceptible shake. Of course

he'd take the easy way out. Why go to the trouble to win a bride and get her pregnant when his former lover had already produced a potential heir. And then there were the two dozen red roses he'd had sent to her office. While grandly romantic, the gesture had barely aroused a twinge of temptation.

It was the vulnerability she'd infrequently glimpsed in him that destroyed all her self-preservation and led to repeated disappointments. During those moments, when his shoulders hunched and the cocky playboy vanished, her defenses crumbled. Whether or not he could accept it, Christian yearned for someone to believe in him, and until he pushed her out of his life, Noelle had naively thought that someone was her.

And now he was back. And making demands on her once more. Concern that Christian had appeared suspicious of her hasty engagement swept over her. Half acting the part of smitten fiancée, half because she needed reassurance, Noelle reached for Geoff's hand. He responded with a tender smile that would have made her heart flutter if she was actually in love with him.

Christian observed their exchange through half-lidded eyes and Noelle was convinced she and Geoff were successfully selling the fabrication. But when the stilted meal at long last concluded, it was Christian's hand, warm and too familiar, at the small of her back as they made their way from the restaurant. Geoff had deferred to Christian's rank, and she was now far too aware that her willpower wasn't as strong as she'd hoped. As she wove between the tables, a slowly expanding coil of heat threatened her peace of mind.

Christian's car and driver awaited him at the curb, but instead of bidding them good-night, he lingered while the valet brought Geoff's car around. They made an awkward trio.

When Geoff would have opened the car door and handed Noelle into the passenger seat, Christian used his height and broad shoulders as a not so subtle barrier to keep Geoff from reaching her.

"I've got this." Christian set his hand on the car door and lifted the corners of his lips, shooting Geoff a perfunctory smile that was quickly gone. When he shifted his gaze to Noelle, his eyes glowed with possessive intent.

"Thank you for a lovely evening," she said as Christian handed her into the passenger seat.

"I enjoyed meeting your fiancé, but we didn't get the chance to talk about Marc or our future. I'll call you tomorrow and we can discuss the best time for the three of us to get together."

Before Noelle could protest, Christian shut the door and with a brief, wicked grin at getting in the last word, backed away from the car.

Geoff glanced at her before pulling away from the curb. "Are you okay?"

"Sure," she lied, tearing her gaze away from Christian with effort. "Why wouldn't I be?"

"He's still watching us go."

Noelle's nerves were frayed by the tension. "How do you expect me to respond to that?" she snapped, her tone harsh. As soon as the words were out she hunched her shoulders. "I'm sorry. The man gets to me."

"From the way he was looking at you tonight, you get to him, as well."

Geoff probably meant for his words to reassure her. Instead, she just barely resisted the urge to drop her face into her hands and moan in misery. The last thing she needed was to speculate whether Christian's interest in marrying her was motivated by anything other than expediency.

"You're supposed to be the sensible voice that tells me

not to get involved with Christian." Noelle sighed, predicting a long sleepless night ahead. "I need to keep my head clear and my emotions on ice until he gives up on the idea of marrying me."

"You don't think he bought that we're madly in love and destined to live happily-ever-after?" Geoff's wry inflection had serious undertones. Earlier that day he'd tried to talk her out of her gambit, but she'd been too panicky to listen.

"Maybe at first."

"I thought I played the part of your ardent suitor very well."

"You did." The flaw in the plan lay solely at her doorstep. How could she pretend to be in love with Geoff if her heart still fluttered when Christian was near? With a woeful sigh she surrendered to the inevitable.

Noelle grasped the enormous diamond and slid the ring from her finger. It was a relief to take the clumsy thing off. She might have handled the weight better if she didn't feel so much regret about dragging Geoff into her schemes.

With one corner of his mouth lifted in a half smile, Geoff took the ring and popped it into his breast pocket. "And just like that I'm a single man again."

"It was my fault he saw through us. I shouldn't have attempted to trick him. He's far too astute for that. He's probably already had you checked out and knows we're not together."

Geoff's expression turned serious. "Your openness and honesty are what everyone loves about you. Don't let Christian turn you into someone you're not. Be honest with him about your fears for Marc."

At the moment Noelle wasn't feeling remotely honest or lovable. She was an anxious mother ready to defend her child through whatever devious or dirty means necessary.

"Are you sure the prince isn't sincere about wanting a relationship with Marc?"

"I don't know." Her heart had a different opinion, but Noelle couldn't trust the poor, misguided thing. "I'd feel better about it if he wasn't under pressure to produce an heir."

For five long years, a tiny, hopeful part of her had been waiting for Christian to appear on her doorstep the way he used to when they were together. Each year her optimism had dimmed until only a minute speck of it remained. Now he wanted back in her life. Not because he missed her or realized she was his soul mate, but because she'd given birth to his son, and Marc was a quick fix for his current predicament.

"You seem to have forgotten that you and Marc are a package deal." Geoff took his eyes off the road and shot her a somber glance. "The only way Marc becomes his heir is if he's legitimate. Which means Christian needs to marry you."

To her shame the thought sent a wanton burst of anticipation ripping through her. The way her stomach clenched was both familiar and unwelcome. She hated her body's involuntary reaction because that meant she was susceptible to the abundant tools in Christian's sexual arsenal.

She extended her hand, palm up. "You're right. Please return my ring. The engagement is back on."

Geoff shook his head, making no move to oblige her. "I'll not be jilted by you twice. You're going to have to sort out your issues with Christian without resorting to any more ill-advised schemes."

# Five

Christian paced before the French doors that led from the green drawing room to the extensive garden at the back of the palace. He tugged his left sleeve down over his watch. During the past fifteen minutes, the movement had become a nervous tick as he'd checked the time every twenty seconds or so. Noelle and Marc were late to the meeting she'd finally agreed to. The waiting was eating away the last of Christian's calm.

He decided to take his agitation out on Gabriel. "I still can't believe you've known that I had a son and didn't tell me."

From his spot on the emerald-colored sofa in the center of the room, the crown prince of Sherdana glanced up from his smartphone, unruffled by his brother's aggressive tone. "Olivia and I suspected. We didn't know for sure. And until the DNA tests come back, you don't, either."

Christian snorted in reply as he continued his path

back and forth across the eighteenth-century carpet. The aimless movement wasn't improving his situation, so he stopped before his brother and scowled at him.

"He's my son. He has the Alessandro eyes and looks the way we did at four." Although the triplets weren't identical, as children they'd been enough alike in appearance to confuse strangers.

"So now you know." Gabriel's lips curved into a challenging smile. "What happens next?"

"I get to know my son."

From the speed with which his brother's attention returned to his phone, Gabriel hadn't approved of Christian's offhanded response. Irritation spread from his chest to his gut.

"What?" he demanded.

"You've always played it just a little too safe where relationships were concerned."

"And you haven't?"

It wasn't a fair criticism. Gabriel had fallen hard for Marissa Somme, the deceased mother of his twin two-year-old daughters. But unlike Christian, Gabriel was first in line to the Sherdanian throne and put duty above all else. From the moment he'd begun the affair with the half-French, half-American model, Gabriel had known it must end. Sherdana's constitution decreed that in order for his son to rule the country one day, the child's mother had to be either a European aristocrat or a Sherdanian citizen.

Marissa had been neither, and Gabriel had ended the relationship. At the time he hadn't known he was going to be a father. That bomb had been dropped on him weeks before he was to marry Lady Olivia Darcy. Her British ancestry made her an exceptional candidate for princess. Or that's the way it had appeared until her fertility issues had made her unsuitable to be Gabriel's wife.

When Gabriel didn't respond to his brother's ineffectual gibe, Christian continued. "What do you want from me?"

"An heir would be nice."

"Nice." Christian practically spit the word. *Nice* didn't describe the pressure his family had put upon him once Gabriel married a woman who could never bear children and Nic had announced his intention to make an American his wife. "You think I should marry Noelle."

That he'd already intended to do just that didn't lessen Christian's annoyance. He was sick of everyone telling him what to do.

"It's about time you put the needs of this family and this country above your own."

"What about Nic? He's been in America for ten years trying to build his damned rocket ship. Why does he get to keep doing what he wants?" Christian immediately regretted his petulant tone, but the resentment he'd kept bottled up for the past three months had a mind of its own.

"If you hadn't played the third-in-line-to-the-throne card like you always do, expecting me or Nic to be the responsible ones, you might have been able to marry the woman of your dreams, suitable or not. Then Nic would be the one ranting and raving about the unfairness of doing his *duty* to Sherdana."

*Duty.*

Christian was getting awfully sick of that word. Until four months ago, the only feeling Christian had about matrimony was utter relief that he'd never be forced down the aisle because the country required it. Producing an heir was Gabriel's obligation as firstborn. Christian enjoyed all the perks of a princely title without any of the demands. And he wasn't beleaguered by guilt over his freedom. If it was selfish of him, so be it.

"We all know I'm not marriage material," Christian

grumbled, casting a glance toward the doorway for the hundredth time. "I wonder what's keeping them."

He was eager to start bonding with his son. And convincing the child's mother that her life would be so much better as his princess. Princess Noelle had a nice ring to it. She might be resistant to the idea of marrying Christian the man, but once she saw how fast doors opened for her as his royal consort, she would realize that Christian the prince was a magnificent catch.

"They'll be here shortly," Gabriel said.

"Do you have some sort of tracking app on your phone that notifies you when guests arrive?" Christian's words were meant to irritate his brother, but the grim, uptight Gabriel of a year ago had been replaced by a relaxed, charming prince of the realm who was impossible to rile.

"No." Gabriel's lips curved in a private smile. "I'm texting with Olivia. She said Marc has finished his third cookie and Mother's ten-thirty appointment has arrived."

Adrenaline zinged through Christian. "Noelle and Marc are already here? How long?"

"About twenty minutes."

"Is that why you're in here with me? To keep me occupied while Olivia introduced Marc to our mother? Did it ever occur to you that I wanted to get to know my son a little before I sprang him on the family?"

"If that's the case, you shouldn't have arranged for him to come here today."

"Noelle suggested it. She didn't want me showing up at her home and bringing media attention with me, and I certainly couldn't spend time with them in public. The palace made sense, since she's been here several times." Christian massaged the back of his neck to ease the stiffness brought on by the stress of his brother's interference. "I thought we could have a quiet couple hours…"

Dammit.

He liked keeping his personal life as far from the palace as possible. While he didn't mind his romantic escapades making a splash in tabloids all over Europe, he'd never once gone out of his way to introduce any of the jet-setters to his family. His friends liked to party. So did he. End of story. Not one of them could have captured the heart of a nation the way Olivia and Brooke had. His women were flashy, spoiled and selfish. Not one wanted a deeper connection. That suited him just fine.

Noelle was the complete opposite. A timeless beauty, her meteoric rise in the world of bridal fashion had captured the media's attention. Every single article Christian had read about her in the past week had praised her vision and talent. They loved how she'd started as an assistant designer at Matteo Pizarro Designs and been mentored by the great man himself. Of course, Christian wasn't surprised by her success. He'd known five years ago that her gift for design would take her a long way. It was her lack of confidence that had held her back.

And her love for him.

"Did Olivia say anything about how the meeting with Mother went?"

With two royal weddings taking place within a couple months of each other, Christian had made himself scarce around the palace, but he was certain Noelle had met the queen during one of her dress fittings with Gabriel's twin girls who'd acted as flower girls for both Olivia and Brooke. Of course, on those occasions she'd been the talented fashion designer who'd crafted the fairy-tale wedding gowns worn by his brothers' brides. As the mother of what might just be the future monarch of Sherdana, she would undergo a vastly different scrutiny. What if the queen decided Noelle wasn't suitable to become a member of the royal family?

And what had the queen thought of her grandson? Would the child pass muster? Christian couldn't rein in his concern. "Did mother like Marc?"

From the way Gabriel's keen gaze rested on him, Christian had failed to sound casual.

"I'm sure Noelle will tell you all about it when she arrives. Olivia is bringing them now."

Christian would have preferred a briefing from an impartial third party like his brother's clever wife, but clamped down on his agitation. Instead, he focused on what he could recall of the boy. Their brief encounter had left him with little more than a series of impressions. Fierce Alessandro eyes. Protective stance. Disapproval of the man his mother had introduced as Prince Christian.

Had Noelle already explained to Marc who Christian truly was? Or did she plan to do so today with Christian at her side? It was a question he probably should have asked his former flame days ago, but Christian hadn't been thinking about how the news might rock the four-year-old's world. He'd been too caught up in how the discovery had impacted him.

"Do you and Olivia plan to stick around for a bit?"

Gabriel eyed him, his expression thoughtful. "We hadn't planned to."

"Would you?" Christian suspected the strain would be muted if he, Noelle and Marc weren't left alone right away. "Just for a bit. Marc might be a bit overwhelmed."

"Yes," Gabriel drawled. "I'm sure it's Marc that we need to worry about."

"If you're implying that I'm anxious…"

It wasn't like Christian to let anyone see him sweat, but maybe just this once it would be okay. If anyone would understand how he felt, it would be Gabriel. Several months ago, Sherdana's crown prince had been surprised in the same way when twin toddlers, Karina and Bethany, had arrived on his doorstep after their mother died. Christian had been impressed how well his brother had adapted to fatherhood. Of course, the girls were two years younger than Marc and probably hadn't yet missed having a father. But a boy was different. He needed a male influence in his life. Someone to look up to.

"I have a four-year-old son I've barely met," Christian murmured, overwhelmed with awe and dismay.

"It's terrifying." Gabriel clapped him on the back, the solid blow knocking Christian away from the brink of panic. "Can't wait to meet him."

As if on cue, a dark-haired boy streaked through the doorway and dodged around several carefully arranged chairs, making a beeline for the enormous fireplace at the opposite end of the room.

"Look, I can fit in this one, too." Dressed in navy pants and a pale blue shirt, Marc stood framed in the white marble surround, arms outstretched and wearing a precocious grin.

The boy's compelling enthusiasm drew and held every adult eye in the room. Christian was the first to look away. Noelle had entered on Olivia's heels, and he stole a moment to drink in her quiet beauty.

In manner and appearance, Noelle was more like Gabriel's graceful, elegant wife than Nic's bohemian spitfire. Today Noelle wore a textured brown sheath with black side panels that accentuated her slender curves. A two-inch ruffled flounce at the hemline boosted the design from simple to striking.

"Marc, come out of there," Noelle scolded with a quick

apologetic glance to where Gabriel stood with his arm wrapped around Olivia's waist.

After four months Christian still wasn't accustomed to his brother's easy affection with his new wife. Even as a child Gabriel had been somber and formal most of the time, as if his future crown already weighed heavily on his head. Christian marveled to see him now, relaxed and smiling as he kissed Olivia on the cheek and whispered something in her ear that brought rosy delight to her cheeks.

Christian tore his gaze from the happy couple in time to catch the wistfulness that softened Noelle's expression as she too regarded the royal pair. A realization tore at him: he wanted the same intimate connection with Noelle that Gabriel had with Olivia. A partnership that sizzled in the bedroom and worked everywhere else.

Pity he'd already betrayed the trust that would permit him to have, either.

Noelle couldn't think straight with Christian and her son in the same room. Given Marc's adverse reaction to Christian the night he'd shown up unannounced, she was worried that her son wouldn't want to have anything to do with his father.

And that was the least of her problems.

Having a meeting with Christian's mother sprung on her had been bad enough, but to then watch her transform from imperious queen to adoring grandmother in the space of ten minutes had made Noelle question her decision to keep Marc's paternity a secret. Now that the truth was out, she expected the pressure to legitimize Marc by marrying Christian would increase tenfold.

Nor did it appear as if she would have a single supporter in the palace if she decided against marriage. Olivia had already said the twins would be so excited when Marc came to live in the palace, and Gabriel was obviously enjoying his nephew's antics. The suspicion Noelle expected to encounter had been nonexistent. Everyone seemed to accept that Marc was Christian's son.

Which meant whatever Noelle chose for her son's future, she had no one to blame but herself for the consequences.

Her eyes hurt with the effort of keeping her gaze from devouring Christian. Whenever he was near, she had to fight to maintain a neutral demeanor. After a five-year drought, spending so much time with him was starting to eat into her willpower. It wasn't fair how easily she regressed into familiar patterns. Back when they were lovers, she used to spend hours beside him in bed, content to work on her designs or lapse into frivolous romanticism and doodle their names, connecting the letters with intricate loops and flourishes. Looking back on it now, Noelle couldn't believe she'd been that foolish.

"Marc," she called, putting aside her memories of past imprudence, "come meet Prince Gabriel."

The little boy gave a green sofa and several chairs a wide berth to avoid Christian before coming to stand at Noelle's side and fixing solemn, unblinking eyes on the handsome, regal man beside Olivia.

Prince Gabriel put his hand out. "Nice to meet you, Marc."

Most four-year-olds wouldn't have known to be awed by the man who would one day rule the country, but Marc had his father's confidence as well as his mercurial temperament.

"Nice to meet you, Prince Gabriel."

Noelle was torn between relief and pride at her son's exhibition of good manners, but she held her breath as he continued to speak.

"I like your palace. It's very large. Do you ever play hide and seek?"

Prince Gabriel's lips twitched at Marc's earnest question, but he gave him a grave reply. "Not for many years. But my daughters are big fans of the game. Perhaps one day you can play with them."

Marc didn't look to Noelle for confirmation before nodding. "I'd like that."

"Would you like to see the garden?" Olivia asked.

Christian stepped up beside his brother. "He might be interested in the stables, as well."

"Are there pumpkins in the garden?" Marc asked, acting as if he hadn't heard Christian. "We have three pumpkins at home, and they're this big." He demonstrated their size with his hands, adding about two feet to the actual diameter.

"No pumpkins, I'm afraid," Olivia said, glancing from Christian to Noelle. "But we have a pond with goldfish."

Noticing Christian's taut expression, Noelle said, "Marc, why don't you let Princess Olivia show you the pond and I'll be out in a little bit."

With an excited roar, Marc raced toward the French doors, Olivia and Gabriel trailing behind. As the trio exited the room, Noelle's tension ratcheted upward. A muscle bunched in Christian's jaw as he tracked Marc's rambunctious dash across the lush, verdant lawn until he was out of sight. At last his hard gaze swung to Noelle.

"What have you said to my son to make him hate me?"

She wasn't surprised by Christian's question. "I haven't told him anything at all about you."

"Not even that I'm his father?"

Noelle sighed. "No, not yet. I've always said that I never told his father about him because I liked our family just as it was."

"And he was satisfied with that?" Christian sounded skeptical.

"He's four. For the moment it's enough." Noelle knew her son's innate curiosity wouldn't allow him to let the matter drop indefinitely. "He doesn't hate you," she added.

"Then why is it he gives me a wide berth?"

"You weren't exactly charming when you showed up unannounced at my home."

"I was upset to discover you'd been hiding a son from me all these years."

"I wasn't hiding him." Noelle blinked in surprise as she took in Christian's bitterness. "You would have known about him if you'd ever bothered to contact me in the months following our breakup." She fumbled over the last word.

His dismissal of her hadn't felt like a true breakup. He hadn't said he was unhappy with their relationship or that he wanted to see other people. He'd just told her to take the job she'd been offered at Matteo Pizarro Designs in Paris. After she'd given him her heart and two years of her life, he'd not been the least bit regretful that she'd be moving so far away nor had he offered to keep in touch.

"See, you are still angry with me," he said, pointing a taunting finger at her. "And you're inferring I didn't want to be a part of his life."

Yes, she'd been hurt by his rejection, but that was five years ago. Granted, it still rankled her, but had she turned her son against his father without meaning to? Uncertainty put her on the defensive.

"You don't know me at all if you think that." The man was an insufferable egotist. "And may I point out that simply by your absence you've become alienated from Marc."

"Did you ever try to contact me?" Christian persisted. "To let me know you were pregnant?"

"To what end? You made it pretty clear you were finished with me." She shook her head, throat contracting in remembered pain. "And if I had, what would you have done? When would you have found time between work and play to be a father?" She was warming to her argument now. "Marc deserves someone who will be there for him all the time not when it fits into his schedule."

"Someone like Coomb?" Christian grabbed her bare right hand and held it up. "Where's your engagement ring, Noelle?"

His strong touch sent a burst of heat through her. She hesitated too long before attempting to tug free. "Geoff and I talked. Given the circumstances, he thinks it would be less confusing for Marc if he stepped out of the picture and gave you and Marc a chance to bond." Chest heaving, she stopped trying to make Christian let her go and stood glaring at him.

"It wasn't much of an engagement if he gave you up so easily." Soft and measured, Christian's remark cut her deep.

"He's concerned for Marc." Geoff had been right about her scheme being a bad idea. It had backfired mightily, and once again Christian perceived her as mundane and unable to inspire a man's passion. "My son loves Geoff. You should appreciate that he was willing to step aside and not complicate an already tricky situation."

Terrified that Christian would see the tears scalding her eyes, she spun away from him and took several steps toward the French doors and the safety of the garden. But she wasn't fast enough and he caught her before she could slip outside.

"I was ready to battle him for you," he murmured, fingers grazing the wet streak on her cheek. "To demonstrate how committed I am to being your ardent husband and a zealous father to Marc."

Such beautiful words from such a challenging and unpredictable man. Noelle couldn't decide whether to laugh or cry. She was still debating when Christian cupped her face in his hands and brought his lips to hers.

The delicious pressure of his kiss held her immobile with shock. She was transported back in time to their first kiss. It had started very differently than this one, in merriment not bitterness. They'd been laughing at something silly, a bit of urban slang she'd used wrong.

In the beginning of their unlikely friendship, Christian had come to her apartment when he was feeling low and out of sorts. He claimed she had a knack for chasing away his shadows, and she was flattered that a charismatic prince, one whose favor was sought by everyone, saw *her* as special.

Noelle tunneled impatient fingers into Christian's hair and pushed her greedy body hard against his. She was starving for physical affection. Being hugged by her son was wonderful, but sometimes she just craved a man's hands on her. To feel a little helpless as he tore off her clothes and had his way with her. And Christian had a knack for this sort of thing. His firm, masterful touch reduced her to quivering need.

His fingers bit into her hip as she rocked against him, the ache between her thighs building. She rubbed her breasts against his chest to ease her yearning, but the friction only caused her to burn hotter.

Men's voices, coming from the direction of the garden, awoke Noelle to the insanity of what she was doing. She broke off the kiss, but hadn't the strength to escape Christian's embrace. Had she lost all sense? Any second they could be discovered by the palace's staff, Christian's family. Her son.

Christian took advantage of her unsteadiness and buried his face in her neck. His lips glided over her skin, leaving a tingling sensation in his wake. "I knew you'd come around."

An icy chill swept through her at his words. Noelle clenched her teeth and cursed her impulsiveness. She tensed and twisted away.

"I haven't come around to anything."

"Ten seconds ago you were melted butter in my arms." He crossed said arms across his formidable chest and lobbed a wolfish grin in her direction. "I'd say that's a pretty good indication that you agree it's better for all of us if we marry."

With her heart pumping gallons of hot, sexually charged blood through her veins, it was a little hard to pretend she was unaffected by their steamy kiss. "Sex was always great between us," she admitted, "but it's not a reason to get married."

"Not the only reason obviously, but wouldn't you be happier with a man who can drive you wild in bed? I do that for you. Why are you fighting this?"

His arrogance left her momentarily speechless. She spent a silent few seconds studying his face. What she saw gave her reason to believe his confidence was at least partially contrived.

"I'm not fighting anything. I'm trying to make a sensible decision based on what's best for Marc and me." Her cheeks heated a little at the skeptical look in Christian's eyes. Okay, plastering herself all over him hadn't been sensible, but to be fair, he had a gift for jazzing her hormones and muddling her judgment. "And being kissed by you isn't making that any easier."

He stretched out his hand and cupped her cheek in his palm. Her wobbly knees hadn't let her move beyond his grasp, and she found herself held in place while he closed the narrow gap and dropped his lips to hers once again. Hard and brief, the kiss affirmed that he respected her admission and wasn't about to back off.

She sighed as his hand slid away. "I really need to go see what Marc is up to."

"Let's go."

Christian refrained from touching her as they exited the room and headed across the lawn in the direction of the koi pond. Longing knotted Noelle's muscles. Already she was too aware of the exact distance from his hand to hers. The expressive nuances of his gold eyes as he darted a glance her way. The heat pooling in her belly as she relived their kiss.

Marc was lying on one of the flat rocks surrounding the pool, his nose inches from the surface of the water as Noelle and Christian approached. Her son's enthusiastic chatter wasn't distracting enough for Noelle to miss the curiosity in Olivia's gaze as it bounced between her and Christian. Unable to stop the rush of heat that suffused her cheeks, Noelle wasn't sure whether she liked the princess's obvious approval. With so many people counting on Christian to produce an heir and Marc waiting in the wings to be legitimized, the pressure on Noelle was mounting.

Would anyone understand if she turned Christian down? Was she wrong to want her son to grow up without the responsibility of ruling a country looming over his head? And was it selfish to take her own feelings into consideration? Christian might be the sort of lover every woman dreamed of, but was he husband and father material? No, based on her past experience with him. But five years had changed her. Could the same be said for him? And how involved was she going to let herself get before she knew for sure?

# Six

Christian stopped on the opposite side of the fishpond from his son and drank in the sights and sounds of the energetic boy from behind a polite mask. His heart continued to drive against his ribs following the encounter with Noelle in the green drawing room. An odd lightness had invaded his head as if he wasn't getting the proper amount of oxygen. Which was ridiculous because he was gathering huge lungsful of air laden with the scents of fresh-cut grass, newly turned earth and Noelle's light floral perfume. He suspected her scent was affecting his equilibrium.

Marc laughed as one of the big orange koi flipped its tail and sent water splashing onto his cheek. "Mama, did you see that? The fish waved at me."

"I saw. Why don't we take a walk to the barn?"

"It should be about time for Bethany and Karina's riding lesson," Gabriel added. "Maybe you'd like to see their ponies?"

"Sure." Marc got to his feet and went to slide his hand into Olivia's. "Will you take me?"

She exchanged a brief, poignant look with her husband and then shook her head. "I'm afraid Prince Gabriel and I have someplace we need to be, but Prince Christian knows the stables inside and out. He can take you."

Olivia and Gabriel said their goodbyes and headed for the palace. Marc watched them go before turning to his mother.

"Can't I just stay here with the fish? I don't care about ponies."

"A second ago you were ready to visit the barn," Noelle pointed out, the skin between her sable eyebrows puckering as she frowned. "And since when don't you like ponies?"

"I'll go if he doesn't come with us."

"That's impolite." Thunderclouds formed in her eyes. "Prince Christian is a very busy man. He is taking time away from his business to spend it with us."

"Can't he just go back to work?"

Noelle's lips firmed into a tight line, and she cast a mortified look Christian's way. Despite being frustrated that he was his son's least favorite person, Christian liked that she was concerned about his feelings.

"First the stables," Christian said, his tone shutting down further argument. "Then I'm going to take you and your mother to lunch at a really wonderful restaurant down by the river." Neither lunch nor being seen together in a public place had been a part of their original plan for the day, but Christian was feeling a little desperate at the moment.

"I'm not hungry." The boy had become sullen.

Christian was not going to give up. "That's too bad because this is a new American-style restaurant that has the best hamburgers and milkshakes in Sherdana." It didn't occur to him that Noelle might not want her son eating the less than healthy food until he noticed she was regarding the slim gold watch on her wrist. "It's okay if we go there, right?" he belatedly asked, giving her a winning grin.

"I wasn't planning on taking time for lunch. I have an appointment in an hour."

"Marc and I could go by ourselves." He smiled at the boy. "And I could drop him off after."

"I suppose that would work. How does that sound to you, Marc?"

The four-year-old dug the toe of his brown loafer into the ground and stared down. "I don't feel good."

Christian recognized a losing battle when he saw one. How was he supposed to get to know his son when the boy didn't want to have anything to do with him? "Perhaps another time then."

"Can we go home, Mama?"

"Of course." Noelle ruffled her son's dark wavy hair and mouthed an apology to Christian. "And straight into bed. That's where sick boys belong."

"But I was supposed to play with Dino this afternoon."

"I'm not sure you'll be feeling better that fast."

Marc aimed a surly glare in Christian's direction, obviously blaming him for the canceled play date, before taking the hand his mother put out to him.

"It was nice seeing you again, Marc." Christian sounded more like a prince and not at all like a father.

The boy said nothing. So, Christian tried a smile, but the muscles around his mouth didn't want to cooperate. His awkwardness around his son made him come off stilted and unfriendly. It wasn't at all like him. Gabriel's two girls adored Uncle Christian. He snuck them sweets and helped them play tricks on their nanny and the maids charged with caring for them. That he wasn't developing the same rapport with his son frustrated him.

"Please say goodbye to the prince," Noelle said.

Her firm prompting produced a grumbled response from Marc. Looking exasperated, Noelle tugged him in the direction of the palace. Christian watched their progress and waited until they'd reentered the building before heading back himself.

He was met halfway by his mother's private secretary. Gwen had been with the queen since the triplets had been born. Despite her sensible two-inch heels, her head barely came as high as Christian's shoulder. Her diminutive size sometimes caused her to be underestimated. No one made that mistake twice.

"The queen would like you to come to her office."

The summons wasn't unexpected. After meeting Marc, she was sure to have questions for Christian. "Right now?" His mother only sent her secretary when she expected immediate results, and the question would irritate Gwen, but he needed to release some steam.

Gwen's eyebrows arched. "You have somewhere more important to be?" So much for riling Gwen.

Christian shook his head. "Lead the way."

"I have things that require my attention. I'm sure you can find your way on your own."

Despite his foul mood, Christian grinned. Perhaps he'd gotten to her after all.

As much as he'd have liked to drag his feet on the way to his mother's first-floor office overlooking the meticulous gardens that were her passion, Christian figured the sooner she spoke her piece, the faster he could get back to the challenge of persuading Noelle and Marc that they should be a family.

"Good morning, Mother," he said as he entered her office and took a seat across from her. "Your gardens look lovely as always. I don't know how you do it."

The queen was not to be distracted by his flattery. "I'm surprised you noticed. It seemed as if your attention was focused on Noelle Dubone and that son of hers." The queen paused and tilted her head, prompting him to answer the unasked question. When Christian remained mum, she continued. "Or should I say that son of yours. You're planning to marry her, I presume. We simply cannot have any more illegitimate royal children running around Sherdana."

"I'm working on that."

"Good. I'd like you to have a ring on her finger before the media gets hold of this. We've had enough scandalous romance at the palace in the past year to last several generations of Alessandro rule. There aren't any other of your progeny running around Europe, are there?"

"Not that I know of." He didn't add that he hadn't known about Marc either, but if he was honest with himself, he hadn't always been as careful with Noelle as he'd been with other women.

His answer did not please his mother one bit. "Christian!"

"No. There aren't."

"How can you be sure?"

"I've been careful."

The queen's expression grew even more severe. "Not careful enough."

"Noelle was different." It was almost a relief to let himself think about her all the time. He'd spent five years pushing her out of his mind. When a bit of music reminded him of slow dancing in her apartment, her body languid against his as his palms coasted along her curves. Or when he'd catch a whiff of the perfume he'd bought her and re-

membered introducing her to several new places to wear
the scent.

"Christian?" His mother's sharp voice jerked him back
from those heady intoxicating days.

"Yes?"

"We need an heir for the throne." She didn't need to add
that he was their last chance to make that happen.

He gave her a short nod. "I'll do whatever it takes to
convince Noelle to marry me." He was more determined
than ever because if Noelle refused him, he wasn't sure
he could marry anyone else.

Noelle's shop was sized to cater to exclusive clients.
Generally the brides arrived with a single assistant or an
entourage of no more than six. Today's appointment was
taxing the salon space. There were twenty opinionated
family members and one browbeaten bride. The youngest
daughter of a billionaire Greek shipping magnate, Daria
was the last of her four sisters to marry, and they all had
advice for their baby sister. Additional guidance was being
provided by two grandmothers, the girl's mother, soon-to-
be mother-in-law and several current and future sisters-
in-law.

In advance of this appointment, Noelle had provided a
dozen sketches in three rounds of correspondence over a
period of two months. The bride or—as was looking more
likely—the bride's family had chosen five of the twelve.
Knowing she wasn't the only designer the bride was looking at, Noelle had pulled out all the stops. The gowns were
elegant, fantasy creations perfect for a twenty-year-old
bride. She looked gorgeous in each and every one.

While her family squabbled over every look, Noelle
could see her designs had not yet resonated with Daria.
The bride's bland expression grew more distant with each

gown. She answered Noelle's questions in an unhelpful monotone. Rather than worrying that a two hundred thousand euro commission was slipping through her fingers, Noelle pondered what would make the young woman happy.

Noelle stood beside the door in the large dressing room while her assistant designer and head of alterations worked together to free her dissatisfied client from the latest frothy wedding dress.

"I have one last dress for you to try," Noelle stated, hoping the startled confusion on her assistant's face hadn't been noticed by the client.

"But I've already tried on the five gowns."

"I decided to make up an additional dress from the sketches I sent you." The gown was the first designed by Noelle based on a get-acquainted interview she'd had with the bride shortly after the engagement was announced. She'd been surprised that the design had been rejected during the first round and couldn't get it out of her head that the style was perfect for Daria. "Are you interested in seeing it?"

"Of course."

To Noelle's delight, a flicker of curiosity sparkled in the girl's dark doe-like eyes. "Wonderful. Calantha, could you please get Woodland Snow." Since each wedding dress had a personality all its own, Noelle named all her gowns.

"That sounds so pretty."

Noelle's spirits lifted at Daria's comment. It was the most animated the girl had been all day.

"I know it's not one of the designs you initially chose," Noelle said, taking over Calantha's role and helping Daria step out of the rejected gown. Handing the dress to the head of alterations, she made a surreptitious shooing gesture. The woman understood. Noelle wanted the bride's attention to be 100 percent on the new design. "But I think you'll find that the dress is much more striking in person than on paper."

The door opened, and Calantha entered with Woodland Snow. Daria's breath caught as she glimpsed the gown and her brown eyes brightened. This was the reaction Noelle had been hoping for.

"It's beautiful," Daria murmured, reaching out to finger one of the organza flowers sewn onto the sheer white overlay. "I remember this dress. It was my favorite."

Noelle bit the inside of her lip to keep from asking the girl why she hadn't fought for the design. She already knew the answer. Reports stated her father was spending upward of eleven million euro on the wedding. Daria was marrying the son of a very wealthy Italian count, and the event promised to make a huge media splash. The wedding dress Daria wore would have to be over-the-top to start tongues wagging, and this gown's beauty was in the details.

Working quickly, Noelle and Calantha slipped the gown over Daria's head and settled it into place. The young bride stood with her back to the three-way mirror to allow for the perfect reveal. First impressions were the strongest, and Noelle wanted the young woman to fall in love all at once.

"Okay, you may turn around."

Daria stared at her reflection. Tears filled her eyes. "It's perfect."

The gown was a single layer of white chiffon sewn with fluttering organza flowers and a scattering of pearls that mimicked clustered berries over a strapless nude liner. The simple boat neckline and capped sleeves drew the eye to Daria's striking bone structure and beautiful brown eyes. The other dresses had overpowered her, emphasizing her youth and inexperience. But as Noelle watched her consider her appearance, Daria's expression took on a look of proud determination.

"Do you want to show your family?"

Daria shook her head. "There is no reason. This is my wedding and I want this dress. They can see it on my wedding day."

Noelle nodded. "I'll send Yvonne in to see what alterations are needed. I'm thrilled we were able to find you the perfect wedding dress."

She excused herself and headed into the room that held Daria's family. With a smile that balanced diplomacy and firmness, Noelle announced that Daria had chosen a dress and was looking forward to surprising everyone with her choice on her wedding day. There was a mixture of surprise and annoyance on the women's faces.

An hour later, the exhausting group was gone, and Noelle dropped into a chair in her now-empty salon. To her delight, the young heiress had paid for the dress herself, declaring that by doing so the only opinion that mattered was her own. Noelle's staff joyously broke out the bottles of champagne reserved for occasions like these and joined their employer in celebrating.

Noelle was halfway through her third glass when the tinkle of a bell announced someone had entered the shop's reception room. Waving her staff back to their seats, she went to speak to their visitor. Two-and-a-half glasses of champagne consumed over an hour and a half were not enough to make Noelle tipsy, but the sight of Christian's imposing presence for the second time in one day made her head spin.

"Christian? What are you doing here?"

"I want you and Marc to join me at my vineyard this weekend."

She frowned as her body reacted positively to his invitation. "That's moving much too quick."

"I'm sorry, but I don't want to spend months and months tiptoeing around. I want to marry you and be Marc's father. He needs to know who I am and that you and I are serious about becoming a family."

Thanks to her nerve-racking encounter with the queen and the Greek bride's chaotic family, Noelle's diplomatic skills were in short supply. "But what if I'm not serious?"

"Come to the vineyard this weekend and let's talk."

"Just talk?" She suspected Christian would love nothing more than to get her horizontal to plead his case. "I'm not the susceptible girl I once was. You won't be able to seduce me into agreeing with you."

"How about if I just seduce you for the fun of it."

She was far more open to this suggestion but couldn't let him know it. "You should concentrate on your son. He is the one you need to win over."

"Are you saying if Marc comes around you'll marry me?"

Noelle shook her head. "It's just not that easy, Christian. I think you deserve a chance to be in your son's life, but I'm not convinced that what's best for him is to have his life turned upside down as the royal heir."

"What if we'd gotten married before Marc was conceived? Would you still feel the same way?"

He hadn't meant for his words to sting, but Noelle had once been very conscious that they came from vastly different worlds, and Christian was less than enthusiastic about inviting her into his.

"Since that was obviously never going to happen, the issue never crossed my mind." Her voice was stiff. Muscles rigid.

Five years ago, being his secret plaything had bothered her more and more the longer they were together. Then the tabloids began publishing pictures of him with the beautiful daughter of a Dutch viscount and speculation gathered momentum that they were on the brink of an engagement. She'd convinced herself to break things off. Christian had disputed the rumors and made love to her with such passion that she forgot all about the outside world for a while longer.

"Noelle." His deep growl of frustration sent a shiver through her. "I was young and foolish when we were together five years ago. I had no idea what I was losing when I let you walk out of my life."

"Let me walk?" Outrage flooded her with adrenaline. "You shoved me out."

Christian snorted. "Hardly. I told you to take a fantastic career opportunity."

"I wanted to stay with you." There, she'd admitted what had been in her heart five years ago. Spoken the words she'd been too afraid to declare the last time she'd seen him.

"You don't think I knew that? But I'd already taken too much from you, and you deserved better." His statement rang with conviction. "I cared about you more than I was willing to admit. Even to myself."

"I can't believe you." If she did, it would undo all the anger and resentment she'd built up over the years and leave her heart open to being hurt again. "You didn't want me around anymore."

"I know it's easy to blame me for the way things ended between us, but you can't truly tell me you were happy near the end."

Noelle shook her head. "No. I wanted what I couldn't have. To be the woman on your arm as well as the one in your bed."

"We tried that and it didn't work out very well, remember?" He was referring to the night of the accident, and the fact that her foolishness had almost gotten him killed.

"I remember. So, what makes you think it will be any better this time?"

"You'll just have to trust me that it will."

# Seven

The luxurious town car slowed as it passed through the quaint village of Paderna, eight rolling miles from Christian's vineyard. Beside him, Noelle stared past her sleeping son at the shops lining the main street visible through the rear passenger window. With each mile they'd traveled, she'd relaxed a little more. And Christian's tension had grown.

"Just a little bit farther now," he murmured, his voice husky from disuse. They'd spoken little during the two-hour ride. After their contentious discussion three days ago, he was loath to bring up anything that might charge the atmosphere in the car and cause further damage to his relationship with either Noelle or their son.

"I forgot how beautiful the wine country is. And so close to Carone."

"Don't you have cousins up near Gallard that you visit?"

"Not in years, I'm afraid. Work keeps me too busy to

travel for fun." She probably wasn't aware of how wistful she sounded.

"Then I'm doubly glad you agreed to join me this weekend. Some time away will do you good."

She patted her briefcase. "This time is for you and Marc to get to know each other. I have several clients to prepare sketches for."

"You'll at least take an hour or so to tour the winery. I'm very proud of it." Although he made millions buying, fixing and selling corporations, his true passion was crafting the finest vintages in all the country.

He'd acquired Bracci Castle and surrounding vineyards six years earlier from Paulo Veneto, a Sherdanian count who had gambled his way deep into debt. As soon as the hospital had released Christian after the accident, he'd come here to hide and recover. At first the plodding country pace had pained him as much as his scorched flesh. Between his many business dealings and his numerous social engagements, he was used to operating at frenetic speed. Needing something to keep his thoughts occupied and off both the pain in his right side and the agony in his heart, he started learning what it took to produce wine.

At the time, the winery was barely breaking even and the wines were abysmal. Christian figured out that the general manager and winemaker were selling the grapes produced by the vineyard and buying inferior ones at half the cost, pocketing the difference. Within a week Christian had fired and replaced them with two men he'd wooed away from the competition. After sinking a ridiculous amount of money into desperately needed new equipment, he'd held his breath and hoped the grapes were as good as promised. The first harvest had gone well, and the wine produced that year won the winery its first award.

"These are all my fields," Christian said, indicating the rows of well-maintained grapevines.

"I remember when you mentioned buying the vineyard. You don't usually hold on to anything for long. Why keep it?"

"The place makes the finest wines in all Sherdana. Why would I want to give that up?"

"So it's a prestige thing." Her tone revealed that his answer had disappointed her. She wanted him to speak the truth not give her flippant responses.

"I have grown fond of the place."

She nodded. "I can't wait to see it."

And he couldn't wait to show it to her. The seven-hundred-year-old castle had a quirky charm so unlike his sleek, sophisticated apartments at the center of activity in Paris and London. His circle of friends thought he was mad to spend any time here. They couldn't figure out how he kept himself entertained without clubs or expensive restaurants. The isolation that had first bothered him was now like a balm to his soul. One he enjoyed too infrequently thanks to his business commitments.

The car rolled through the arch and beneath the portcullis that was the only way into the castle's outer courtyard. Where in medieval times this large area would have been cobbled, Christian had turned the space into a grassy lawn with paths. The car followed the circular driveway and stopped outside the keep's arched double doors. As the driver got out and opened Christian's door, several staff flowed out of the imposing stone building and headed toward the car. Christian hesitated before sliding out and turned to Noelle. Marc was starting to stir in his car seat.

"Why don't you let me carry him into the house," Christian offered, hoping the child would be less likely to protest since he was drowsy.

"Of course." Noelle exited the car behind him and stood looking up at the towering stone structure in front of her. "This really is a castle, isn't it?"

"What were you expecting?"

She wrinkled her nose. "Something more fairy-tale-like."

Christian chuckled. "It is a hulking brute of a thing, isn't it? Don't worry. You'll like what I've done to the inside. It has running water and electricity."

"No heated buckets of water hauled up from the kitchen and winding stairwells lit by torches?"

"You sound disappointed." It was good to banter with her. The repartee erased the years of separation and recalled why they'd once enjoyed each other's company so much.

"There's a part of me that is."

With his mood growing lighter by the second, Christian unbuckled his son from the car seat and lifted the boy in his arms. The weight of Marc's sleepy head on his shoulder filled Christian with blazing joy. Holding his child was such a simple thing. How many fathers didn't give it a second thought? For Christian the moment was precious, and he closed his eyes to imprint the memory, after which he followed Noelle inside.

The entry hall was a wide room that ran for twenty feet on either side of the front door with a fireplace on each wall. Here they were met by a handsome woman in her midfifties wearing a simple navy dress and a tasteful silver brooch in the shape of a lily.

"Noelle, this is Mrs. Francas, my housekeeper. Whatever you need, you may ask her."

The brunette smiled in welcome. "Ms. Dubone, how lovely to have you and your son staying with us. I will have your bags sent to your rooms. As Prince Christian stated, anything you need, please let me know. We look forward to making your stay extra special in the hopes you'll return."

When Noelle's eyes widened in surprise, Christian cocked his head at Francas's not-so-subtle hint. She'd been Christian's favorite nursemaid when he, Gabriel and Nic were growing up, and as such he gave her a little more latitude when she voiced her opinions than he might have with someone else.

"Thank you," Noelle murmured with a friendly smile.

They entered the great hall. In its heyday everyone in the castle would gather there for meals. The lower section of the thirty-foot walls was lined with dark wainscoting, and enormous paintings depicting hunt scenes were hung above.

"I feel a little bit like I've been transported back to the fourteenth century."

"When I bought the castle, it was in pretty bad shape. Veneto hated the country and rarely spent time at his estate. The stone floors were chipped and uneven. Plaster was crumbling everywhere. I decided to take some of the walls back to the original stone. Where the paneling was in better shape, it was restored."

"Oh!" she exclaimed, pointing at several suits of armor that stood at attention on one end of the room. "Marc is going to love those."

Hearing his name seemed to rouse him. Marc lifted his head from Christian's shoulder and blinked blearily. "Mama?"

"We're at Prince Christian's castle. Look at how big this room is."

Marc's eyes went wide as he gazed around. "Wow." He squirmed a little as he swiveled to check out the space in every direction, but made no attempt to get away from Christian.

Deciding to give up while he was ahead, Christian set down his son. "Go check out that armor over there." He pointed at a set with intricate gold filigree that looked too ornate to have ever been worn into battle.

"Is it yours?" For a couple seconds hero worship blazed in Marc's burnished gold eyes, and Christian reveled in his son's admiration. "Have you ever worn it?"

"No. It was made specially for one of my ancestors and only fit him," Christian explained.

"Did he wear it in battle with trolls?"

"Ah, no." He shot a questioning glance toward Noelle.

"One of his friends has an older brother who is into fantasy novels and likes to tell his brother and Marc all about them."

Christian nodded his understanding. "My great-great-great-great grandfather wore it to defend Sherdana's borders." He had no idea if that was true, but he suspected one of his ancestors had worn the armor, and the story had captured his son's interest.

"Neat."

To Christian's delight Marc was demonstrating none of his usual displeasure when his father was around. While the boy raced from the armor to the display of swords and battle-axes, Christian set his hand in the small of Noelle's back and guided her toward the salon. Here, carpet stretched the length of the stone floor, and paneling covered the rustic walls. Long windows, framed in royal blue velvet, overlooked the castle's inner courtyard. Late-afternoon sunshine fell upon the last of the summer roses. There was a cozy sitting area with wing chairs and a plush sofa before the large fireplace.

"This is where I spend most of my time when I'm here. The stairs—" he gestured to his right "—lead to the first floor and several guest rooms. I can have my housekeeper show you to your rooms now or…"

He hadn't thought much past getting Noelle and Marc here.

"Or?" Noelle prompted, fixing him with a curious stare.

Christian laughed. "I have no idea. How do you feel about exploring outside? There are some terrific views of the countryside from atop the walls."

"I think Marc would love that."

With their son racing ahead of them, Christian and Noelle strolled side by side through the courtyard and up a set of stairs that led to the battlements. The autumn sunshine heightened the greens and golds of the fields surrounding the castle. A light breeze blew Noelle's silky dark hair around her face and tugged at the floral scarf knotted about her slim neck. Christian stroked a strand of hair off her cheek and noticed the way her lashes fluttered at his touch.

Gripped by the desire to take her in his arms and kiss her soft, full lips, Christian trailed his fingertips down her neck and around to her nape. Her faint sigh was nearly his undoing. Only awareness of Marc running back and forth across the battlements, chattering about the height of the walls and pretending he was shooting arrows at the enemy below, kept Christian from acting on the impulses driving through his body. But it didn't keep him from talking about it.

"I think I'm going to go crazy waiting to taste you," he murmured close to her ear, near enough to feel the way her body started at the hot brush of his breath against her skin.

"I can't make any promises until I see how Marc settles down tonight." She peered at Christian from beneath long, sable lashes. "But I very much want to get my hands on you, as well."

His body reacted predictably to her bold remark. Heat poured into his groin while his muscles tightened in delicious anticipation. She left him breathless and off his game. He slid his fingers around her waist and drew her against his side while his lips grazed her temple.

"No one has ever gotten to me the way that you do." Before hunger overrode his willpower, he set her free and raked both hands through his hair. "What changed your mind?"

"I haven't."

"But you just said…" He regarded her, his brain blurry with confusion, wondering what to make of her secretive smile.

"That I've given up trying to fight the chemistry between us. I want to make love with you. It's all I thought about the entire trip here, but I long ago discovered, sex with you does not necessarily mean we have a future."

Noelle hadn't meant the remark to be cruel, but he had to understand where she was coming from. "I'm sorry if that sounded harsh."

"Don't be sorry. I had that coming. You're right. When we were together before, I had no intention of giving up my freedom. I lived in the moment and enjoyed being irresponsible and egocentric."

His words rang with regret, but Noelle wasn't sure he'd changed all that much. "And yet without the actions of your brothers putting you in the difficult position of being the only one who can produce an heir for the throne, you wouldn't be here with Marc and me this weekend."

The truth weighed heavy on her heart. But it didn't stop her from wishing he wanted her and Marc in his life simply because he cared about them. When she tried a smile, the corners of her mouth quivered with the effort of appearing poised and understanding.

"I'm not as bad as you think I am."

"You misunderstand me. I don't think you're bad. I just don't want you to think it's unreasonable for me to doubt your sincerity."

"What does that mean?"

"Be truthful. You want to have sex with me and hope that I will fall back in love with you so we can marry and you can fulfill your obligation to Sherdana."

"You make me sound like a coldhearted bastard." He glared down at her. "Yes, I want us to have sex. Making love to you remains the most inspiring, mind-blowing pleasure I've ever had with any woman. Was I a fool to push you out of my life and give that up? Of course. But I was stupid and afraid, and at the time it seemed like the best thing to do."

Noelle's breath lodged in her chest at his passionate declaration. She could believe that he valued their physical intimacy as much as she had. Although she'd been relatively inexperienced where men and sex were concerned, Christian had been as susceptible to her touch as she'd been to his.

"This is all so complicated," she murmured, her gaze trailing after Marc as she tried to remind herself where her priorities lay.

"It doesn't have to be."

Christian took her hand and squeezed with firm tenderness. Then he lifted it to his face and grazed the inside of her wrist with his lips. Noelle's full attention returned to Christian. Inside she shivered half in terror, half in delight. But when he gave her a smile of heartbreaking gravity, her heart skipped a beat.

Was he right? Should she just forget past disappointments and focus on the future? Once upon a time she would have given anything to marry Christian. Would she have cared if he only wanted her for the child she carried?

No.

She would have wanted her son to know his father and claim his birthright. Being afraid of getting hurt again was not a valid reason to keep Christian and Marc apart.

Noelle gathered a deep breath. "After dinner we should tell Marc you're his father. If we let this drag out much longer, he's going to be very confused that we didn't tell him sooner."

"I'd like that."

They completed the circuit of the battlements and headed back inside the castle to clean up before dinner. Marc was covered in dirt, but Noelle judged him too wound up to attempt a bath. Instead, she washed his hands and face and urged him into clean clothes before leaving him occupied with a game on her tablet so she could freshen up and change for dinner.

Noelle pulled out of her suitcase a simple black V-neck sheath made of rayon, with enough spandex to allow the material to mold to her modest curves. Diagonally placed black piping created interest on what could have been a forgettable dress. Over it she slipped a sheer black short-sleeve cropped jacket ornamented with clusters of downy black feathers. Peep-toe pumps completed the outfit. Noelle felt confident and sexy. Ready to match wits with Christian.

With her son racing down the corridor ahead of her, Noelle made her way back to the ground floor. Christian met her at the bottom of the stairs, looking dashing in a dark gray suit and a crisp white shirt. In a nod to country informality, he'd gone without a tie and left the top button of his shirt undone to expose the strong column of his throat.

Although she'd thought herself calm and sophisticated enough to take Christian to bed without succumbing to feverish, emotional drama, the man was so damned charismatic her heart fluttered wildly the instant their eyes met. Parts of her came to glorious life at his slow, deliberate grin. He would not let her withdraw her admission that she wanted them to make love. A heavy ache began low in her belly. She craved his hands on her. Judging from the heat blazing in his eyes, before the night was out he intended to make that happen.

But first, they had to get through a difficult conversation after dinner. Noelle knew by telling Marc the truth she was setting them on a path neither might be ready for. Never before had a meal dragged on the way dinner with Christian and Marc did. If Noelle's thoughts hadn't been in such turmoil, she might have been able to enjoy the excellent lamb chops and the decadent chocolate dessert. As it was, the food barely registered. She listened with half her attention to Christian's attempts to draw out Marc. He had regressed from his earlier friendliness on the battlements back to wariness.

After dinner Noelle guided her son into the salon where one of the maids had placed a pot of coffee. Christian's face showed none of the anxiety Noelle was feeling as she sat her son on the sofa before joining him on the soft cushions.

"Marc, I have something important to tell you about Prince Christian."

Her son squirmed as if fidgeting could somehow let him escape the sudden tension in the room. Noelle set her hand on his knees to stop him from kicking his feet against the sofa frame.

"What?" He slid down so his back was flat against the seat cushions and he was staring up at the coffered ceiling.

Noelle could tell she was losing her son and spoke

quickly. "I wanted to wait until you were old enough to understand."

As if paying no attention to her words, Marc let his body go limp and slid onto the floor. "Did you see that, Mama?"

"I did. Now please come sit on the sofa and listen to what I'm telling you." Her temper rarely flared with Marc, but the past ten days had left her emotions raw and her nerves frayed. She waited until Marc had flopped back into his original seat before setting her hands on his forearms and compelling him to look at her. "Prince Christian is your father."

"No." Marc shook his head hard enough to dislodge the controlled waves his mother had combed his hair into before dinner. "I don't have a father."

"You do. And he's Prince Christian."

Marc got to his knees and leaned close to whisper in her ear. "But I don't like him."

"Of course you do." She aimed a glance at Christian to see how he was reacting.

As if taking this as an invitation, he hunkered down beside his son and offered an engaging smile. Noelle's insides melted at his earnest warmth, but Marc wasn't swayed.

"I don't like him. I like Geoff."

"Just because you like Geoff doesn't mean you can't like your father, too."

"He's not my father. I don't know him."

"I'd like to change that," Christian said. "You and your mom can come stay at the palace, and we'll all get to know each other."

"I don't want to stay at the palace. I want to stay in my house." Marc's face grew red as his frustration grew. "Please, Mama. Can't we stay at our house?"

Noelle hated seeing her son upset and shook her head

at Christian. "It's a lot for him to absorb all at once. Why don't I take him up to bed? We can talk more tomorrow."

Christian ran his large hand over his son's dark hair, looking unsurprised but bleak when the boy flinched and pressed his face against his mother's chest.

"Of course." Christian got to his feet. "Given how we were doing earlier, I had hoped that would have gone better."

"As did I." Noelle dropped a kiss on Marc's head and stood. "Good night, Christian."

Heart heavy, she led her son upstairs to his bedroom where she urged him into his pajamas and found where the maid had put his favorite dragon when she'd unpacked his suitcase.

"Mama, you're not going to let Prince Christian make us live at the palace, are you?" Marc's plea carried less defiance than he'd shown downstairs.

"Not if you don't want to." She lifted the covers, indicated he should get into bed, and then fussed with the sheets and comforter while she sought for some way to convince her son it was all going to be okay. "But I think you might like the palace. You have grandparents, and an uncle and aunt and two cousins who will love spending time with you."

"I only want you and Nana."

What was really going on with Marc? He was usually excited to experience new things. He'd rushed into his first day of school without once glancing back at his mother. An extrovert like his father, he made friends easily.

"You know that Nana and I aren't going anywhere, right?"

Marc sat up and hugged his mother, his arms showing a desperate sort of strength. "Don't make me live with him."

"You don't like the prince?"

"He's okay." Marc sat back down and toyed with his dragon. "Do you like him?"

"Yes, of course." Noelle sensed there were more questions to come and wondered where her son's thoughts were taking him.

"Are you going to marry him?"

With all the time she and Geoff had spent together, Marc had not once asked her that question. Why did he think things were different between her and Christian? Had he overheard them talking, or was it just a logical progression because Christian was his father and in Marc's mind, parents were married?

"I don't know."

"Do you want to?"

Noelle chose her words carefully. "Not if you don't want me to."

Marc took a long time to think about his answer. At last he gave her a solemn nod. "I'll sleep on it." It's what his grandmother often said to him when he asked for something out of the ordinary.

Hiding a smile, Noelle leaned down and kissed her son on his brow. "I'll await your answer in the morning."

After reminding her son that she was right next door, Noelle departed Marc's room. She left the door cracked so the light from the hallway could flow across the soft carpet. They were in a strange place and occasionally he didn't sleep straight through until morning. She didn't want him to wake up to total darkness and get upset.

In her own room, she changed into her favorite ice-blue nightgown and picked up her sketchbook. Finding time to be creative these days was harder and harder as the practical needs of her growing business occupied her more every month. She had employees to supervise and financial data to keep track of. Fabric came in wrong or late. Equipment broke. Clients changed their minds. A hundred details demanded her attention every day.

With a weary sigh, she sat on the window seat that overlooked the inner courtyard and flipped to a blank sheet. For a long moment she stared at the empty page, her mind playing over the conversation she'd just had with her son.

Did she want to marry Christian? If she spoke with her heart, then the answer was a resounding yes. But she'd grown jaded in the past five years and more often chose to follow her head. It kept her from making mistakes and being hurt.

So if she was thinking and not feeling where Christian was concerned, why had she admitted to wanting to make love with him tonight? Heat flooded her core. She shifted on the comfortable cushion, but there was no escaping the pressure between her thighs. Her nightgown's cool silk caressed her flushed skin. Breath quickening, Noelle closed her eyes and let her thoughts drift from one erotic image to another.

A while later, Noelle glanced at the clock, surprised to see an hour had passed. She always lost track of time when Christian occupied her thoughts.

Noelle set aside her sketchbook. She pinned up her hair before slipping into the robe that matched her nightgown. She knew the way to Christian's room. He'd made certain of that when showing her which rooms she and Marc would use during the weekend. Feeling like the heroine in a gothic novel, Noelle moved swiftly along the forbidding stone corridors of the keep. Her light footsteps made little sound on the carpet, but to her sensitive ears, she could have been an entire marching band. By the time she reached Christian's door, her thudding heart and rapid breathing betrayed both nerves and excitement. She took a second to compose herself before knocking.

Wearing pajama bottoms and a scowl, Christian threw open the door as if he intended to shout at whoever had interrupted him. In an instant his annoyance vanished. "Noelle?"

"I'm sorry how Marc took the news that you're his father."

Christian's gaze flicked over her precarious updo, silk robe and bare feet. "You came here dressed like that to talk about Marc?"

"No." She put her hand on his bare chest, savoring the warmth and power of him for a split second before pushing forward. "I just thought it sounded like a more civilized opening than *I want you naked and inside of me before either of us knows what hit us.*"

Taking two steps backward, he gave way before her determined advance. Then his long fingers snagged in the belt that held her robe closed and he tugged her hard against him. She reveled in his passion, anticipation searing along her nerve endings. But as his lips neared hers, she turned her head aside. His breath stroked along her cheek.

"First we need a few ground rules," she murmured, fighting to keep her voice even as his fingers slipped her belt free and parted the robe.

"Ground rules?"

His hot breath against her ear made her shiver.

"This is about sex and nothing more. It doesn't mean I've changed my mind about doing what's best for my son, and it's not a promise that anything will happen between us in the future."

"You're pretty bossy for a half-naked woman."

Her robe fell to the ground, and Noelle gulped as his palms grazed over her silk-clad hips and up her spine. "Just sex," she repeated, her voice a hoarse rasp.

"So this is okay?" He cupped her breast, fingers playing over her rapidly hardening nipple while he watched her expression from beneath thick black lashes.

"Yes."

"And this?" His free hand dislodged the pins in her hair. He sank his fingers into the thick mass that fell around her shoulders and tugged to drag her head back and expose her throat.

Noelle forgot to breathe as he placed his mouth over the pulse in her neck and sucked. Her heartbeat shifted into an erratic rhythm. "Sure."

"So this isn't off-limits?" Moving with slow tormenting precision, his hand left her breast and glided down over her belly to cup her, the heel of his hand applying the perfect pressure to weaken her knees.

"Yes." She barely got the single syllable out before he began pulling his hand away. Frantic, she grasped his wrist and held him in place.

"But you said…"

"I meant no."

"Ah." The word sighed out of him. "I'm going to take you to bed now."

"Lovely."

She was off her feet an instant later.

# Eight

Christian lowered Noelle onto the bed and stepped back to regard her. He'd seen her naked before. Made love to her too many times to count. But for some reason, every time held a special fascination for him. Bracing his hand on the mattress beside her, he trailed his fingers along her skin at the edge of the nightgown. When he reached one of the thin straps that held the gown up, he nudged it off her shoulder.

There was curiosity, not wariness, in Noelle's eyes as she watched him. Uneasiness tangled with desire in his gut. Did she have any idea how the glimpse of one pink nipple peeking above the neckline of her nightgown made him crazy? Her power over him was complete. He would do whatever she asked, give himself over to her pleasure and wait to take his own until she was thoroughly spent.

His erection pulsed as she slid the straps down her arms, taking the bodice with it. As if understanding his weakness, she shimmied the blue silk over her hips and kicked it off. Naked, she lay before him, her gaze confident and direct as she waited for his next move.

"Gorgeous." He ran shaking hands through his hair, savoring the moment. He'd waited five long years to make love to her again, and he'd be damned if he'd rush. "I've missed you."

She sat up and hooked her fingers in the waistband of his pajamas. "Then what's taking you so long to get started?"

The cool air against his naked flesh did little to reduce the heat pulsing through him. He stepped out of his pajama bottoms and caught Noelle's wrists before her fingers could close around him. Putting her hands around his neck where they'd be safely out of the way, he leaned down to take her lips in an explosive kiss.

Together they fell to the mattress. He lay on his back with her draped over him. His hands were free to roam her body at will. Skin like the smoothest satin slipped against his fingertips. Her body was perfect, not because she didn't have flaws but because he never viewed her with a critical eye. Long lean lines of sleek muscle balanced with graceful curves and small, round breasts. Too short to walk a runway, she was his ideal height. In heels, her forehead reached no higher than his lips.

He was kissing her when the need to have her beneath him struck. She gripped his hair as they rolled, laughing until he nipped at her exposed throat. Her back arched as he moved lower and pulled one hard nipple into his mouth.

"Christian." She panted his name as his fingers began their slow descent to the heat between her thighs.

"Yes, Noelle?"

Blood rushed to his groin as he found her wet and ready. Trembling at the effort of keeping his pace easy and unhurried, he slipped a finger around the knot of nerves and felt her shudder.

"Torture," she murmured, but the smile playing at the corners of her mouth told him she didn't mind.

He kissed his way toward her second breast, determined to give it equal and fair treatment. "You sound agitated. Do you wish me to stop?"

"No." She shook her head and lifted her hips as he trailed his fingers down the inside of her thigh to her knee. "I want more."

"More of this?" He swirled his tongue around her nipple and felt her fingers tighten in his hair. "Or...?"

Her head thrashed from side to side as he traced the seam between her thighs. Delighted to see he had her full attention, he slipped one, then two fingers inside her, touching the sensitive spot the way he knew she loved and watching her muscles tense with pleasure. Within seconds she came apart beneath his hands. He savored her every cry and quake, and was a little shocked at the speed and intensity of her orgasm.

As she lay with her eyes closed, her chest heaving with each uneven breath, he reached into his nightstand and pulled out a condom. When he turned back to her, he found her up on one elbow, watching him with glowing eyes. Her pale skin wore the rosy flush of climax, and she looked ready and eager for round two.

Happy to oblige her, Christian slid on the condom and leaned down to snag her gaze with his. "This time we'll come together," he promised and at her nod, positioned himself between her thighs.

Still not fully recovered from one orgasm, but eager to have Christian inside her, Noelle opened for him and felt him nudge against her. Anticipation tightened her nerves to bowstrings, and she told herself to let go. Instead, her body tensed still more. Panic grew as a myriad of half-hysterical what ifs bombarded her mind.

"Easy." Christian's soothing tone lessened her anxiety. "There's no rush."

That's where he was wrong. She needed the rush of passion to keep her brain disengaged. Thinking about what she was doing led to her questioning the wisdom of coming here tonight.

"I'm sorry. It's just…"

While Christian hadn't been her first lover, he'd been her last. For five years she'd concentrated on her son and her career, putting her personal life on ice.

Christian backed off and peered down at her. "Relax. It's fine." He caressed her disheveled hair back from her cheeks with gentle strokes of his fingers. "Talk to me."

"It's been awhile." The flush in her cheeks stopped being about passion and became embarrassment.

Wonder softened the aristocratic planes of his face. He cupped her face with his hands and forced her to meet his gaze. "Then we'll take it very slow."

His lips trailed over her cheek and found a corner of her mouth. She tipped her head to kiss him, but he'd already moved to nuzzle against the sensitive skin beneath her jawline. She closed her eyes and shifted position to offer him better access, shivering as the faintest brush of his lips tickled her skin.

"Touch me," he murmured. "You know what I like."

His words made her smile. She did indeed. She'd clutched his biceps when he'd moved between her thighs, but now, with his encouragement, she let her hands roam. Down his sides, across his tight abs. Her fingertips rode the ridges and valleys of his superb muscles. So much leashed power all hers.

He kissed her then, his lips moving over hers with mastery and controlled passion. He was letting her set the pace. Granting her the time to adjust to being loved by his hands and mouth. Almost immediately her body quickened. Uncertainty fell away. She wrapped her arms around his shoulders and tilted her hips to find his erection waiting for her.

"You know what I need," she whispered, rocking against him, feeling him slide through her slick folds and probe her entrance.

"Are you sure you're okay?"

"Never better."

He rocked forward, easing his way into her with smooth, gradually deepening thrusts. While her mind had blocked all awareness of her arousal, her body had its own agenda. She expanded to welcome Christian's possession and cried out in pleasure as he seated himself fully inside her. With barely a pause, he withdrew, and together they found a familiar rhythm.

How had she forgotten how perfectly they fit together? Bodies attuned, hands knowing exactly how and where to touch—their movements were so perfectly choreographed they could've made love the night before.

Christian's steady thrusts intensified the pleasure building in her body in the same way his rough, unsteady breathing and whispered words of encouragement and praise made her heart sing. Once again Noelle's climax claimed her fast and hard. As aware of her body's reactions as he was of his own, Christian timed his own orgasm so perfectly that they came at nearly the same moment.

In the aftermath, Noelle lay panting and dazed beneath Christian's weight, glad she'd been rational enough to be able to forget this bliss these past five years. Only by focusing on what had been bad about their relationship rather than recalling the good had she learned to live without him. And now he was back. And so were her memories of how amazing his lovemaking had been.

As soon as Christian shifted to lie beside her, Noelle scooted off the bed and made a beeline for her nightgown and robe. She was almost to the door before Christian spoke.

"You're leaving?" He'd levered himself onto his elbows and stared at her in blank shock.

"I think it's best."

"But we haven't talked." He frowned. "And you used to like to snuggle after we made love." He sounded so put out that she had a hard time repressing a smile.

She reached behind her for the door handle. "Yes, well, I don't want to give you the wrong impression."

That brought him to a sitting position. Looking adorable with his hair mussed and his strong, broad shoulders slumped, he asked, "What sort of wrong impression?"

"Sex with you I can handle," she explained, echoing what he'd once said to her. "But I can't do intimacy."

Then before he could rise from the bed to challenge her bold declaration, she slipped out of the room.

Shortly after dawn the next morning, Noelle woke facedown in her own bed, and her first emotion was relief. She stretched her arms and legs, luxuriating in the cool sheets and the unfettered peace of early morning. As amazing as the previous night with Christian had been, she wasn't prepared to dive back into the intimacy of sleeping in his arms and being roused by his morning erection and sensual kisses.

Her skin prickled at the thought, and she smiled in memory of his shocked and worried expression when she'd blithely slipped out of bed after what had been the best sex of her life. If he'd had any clue how shaky her legs had been, he might not have let her go without an encore. Instead, exhausted by her long and stress-filled work week and abundance of exercise both on the battlements yesterday afternoon and in Christian's bed last night, she'd enjoyed a blissful six-and-a-half hours of deep, restful sleep.

She'd barely finished heaving a deep, contented sigh when her bedroom door opened and the slap of four-year-old feet sped across the tile floor. A second later a small body landed on the mattress beside her, and Noelle rolled over to scoop her son into a snug embrace.

"Morning, dumpling," she cooed in his ear, savoring the squeeze of his strong arms around her neck. "Did you sleep well?"

"I dreamed I was a dragon who ate everyone in this castle."

"Even me?" She prodded him in the ribs and tickled him.

Marc writhed and giggled. When she let him gather a breath, he said, "No, Mama. I wouldn't eat you." He gave her a smug grin. "But I ate Prince Christian."

"Your father," she corrected, forcing a light note into her voice. "I don't know that it's polite to eat one of your parents."

"It's okay, Mama. He didn't mind."

Noelle decided not to belabor the point. "Are you hungry? What do you think they'll have for breakfast?"

"Waffles?" Marc asked, his eyes round with hope.

"I don't think they'll have those."

"I can make a special request to the cook," said a deep voice from the direction of the hall. Christian stood framed in the open doorway Marc had come through only moments before. "I'm sure she would be happy to whip up a batch."

Christian looked so handsome in khaki pants and a crisp white shirt with sleeves rolled up to expose his strong forearms. His unexpected appearance when her defenses were down sent her emotions flipping end over end. Somehow she managed a friendly smile. If she'd thought sex with Christian would simplify her feelings for the man, she was a fool.

"We wouldn't want her to go to any trouble."

"I'm sure she wouldn't mind." Christian surveyed her disheveled hair and bare shoulders and she blushed.

"Waffles." Marc crowed the word happily and tried tugging her off the bed. "Get up, Mama. I'm hungry."

"I'll go and arrange it. How long will it take you and Marc to get ready?"

"Half an hour?"

"Are you sure that's enough time?" Christian gave her a slow, complex smile that would take her hours to unravel. "I don't want you to feel rushed."

"It's fine."

With Christian lingering half in and half out of her room, Noelle wasn't inclined to ditch the covers and let him drink his fill of her in the clingy silk nightgown. That he'd seen it last night and much more besides didn't mean she wanted to parade before him in the light of day.

"Marc, why don't you go to your room and get dressed?" she said. "I put out your clothes last night. Don't forget to brush your teeth."

Her son scampered to do as she asked, but although Christian stepped aside to let him past, he showed no interest in withdrawing. In fact, he took a single step into the room. Having a man in her bedroom wasn't something Noelle was used to. Back when she and Christian had been lovers, she'd grown comfortable with being nude around him. But since Marc had come along, she'd fallen into the habit of conservative modesty. The only time she left her bedroom wearing just her nightclothes was in the middle of the night when Marc was a baby or if he had an infrequent nightmare.

"Shouldn't you be getting up, too?" Christian asked.

Noelle bit back a tart retort and slid out of bed. As the cool morning air found her bare skin, she shivered and reached for the silk robe that matched her nightgown. She moved with more haste than grace as she slipped her arms into the sleeves. Last night's confident vixen had been an illusion of shadow and lamplight.

"Don't you need to check with your cook about Marc's waffles?" She wanted him to go and take his penetrating gaze with him. The longer he stared at her, the more her poise suffered.

"As soon as you come here and give me a kiss."

She wrinkled her nose at him. "I haven't brushed my teeth, and I'm far from presentable."

"Do you think I care?" His velvet voice bore a trace of steel. "Come here."

Her muscles moved of their own accord, setting her on a direct path into his waiting arms. As she crossed to him, the glow of his smile thawed her chilled limbs. A second later, his warm hands slipped around her waist and the ardent pressure of his fingers pulled her snug against his unyielding torso. Abruptly impatient, she lifted up on her toes to bring her lips into contact with his sooner.

The kiss was hot and fast. Electricity arched between them, the voltage off the scale. Noelle's body came to instant life, and she moaned beneath Christian's mouth.

Almost as fast as she'd ridden desire upward, she was crashing back to earth. She couldn't let Marc see her and Christian locked in a passionate embrace, so she broke off the kiss and pushed her palms against the unyielding granite of his shoulders.

"Marc mustn't…" She sucked in much-needed air to clear her head.

"Damn." Christian stepped back. Chest heaving, he blinked several times before he managed to focus his gaze on her. "Noelle…"

She had no idea what he intended to say. Nor apparently did he because he merely stared at her for a long, silent moment and then shook his head as if to clear it.

"You said something about checking on breakfast," she prompted, overjoyed to see that the kiss had rattled him. Before last night he'd always been the one in control. His masterful seduction had swept her along. Past comfort zones and pride, reducing her every defense to ashes while he kept his thoughts private. "Waffles?"

"Waffles." With a brief nod he turned away, but before he left he spoke over his shoulder. "Take your time. I'll send one of the maids to check on Marc." And then he was off, striding down the hallway.

Noelle leaned against the heavy wood door, taking stock of the graceless lethargy in her limbs and the fanciful fluttering of her heart. She touched the tip of her tongue to her lips, noting they were still tender from last night's fervent kisses.

She closed her bedroom door and headed for the bathroom, determined to enjoy a long hot shower. Catching sight of her reflection, she noticed the invigorating start to her morning had put a smile on her face. The urge to hum surprised her, and she pushed aside the rational side of her brain that wanted to squash all her reckless joy. Monday morning would be soon enough for her return to cold reality. Until then she intended to see where this new beginning with Christian would take them.

\* \* \*

Christian was still cursing his lack of control around Noelle as he reached the ground floor. As if summoned by his thoughts, Mrs. Francas popped into his line of sight and he stopped short.

"Is it possible for waffles to be served for breakfast?"

"Cook has a new recipe she will be happy to show off."

"And could you send one of the maids to check on Marc? I told Noelle we would take care of him this morning."

"Of course. I will send Elise." Mrs. Francas bowed. "There's coffee and this week's paper waiting for you in the salon."

"Thank you."

After his sleepless night, Christian was ready to consume an entire pot of the strong black stuff his cook brewed. The local paper awaited him beside the silver coffee service. When he came to Bracci Castle, he enjoyed immersing himself in the country life and unplugging from the world at large. Some trips he was more successful than others. Multimillion-dollar business deals rarely went smoothly. This weekend, however, he'd warned his assistant not to bother him with anything short of total bankruptcy.

He needed his complete focus on winning over Marc and demonstrating to Noelle that he was ready to be a father and a husband. Yesterday had been an emotional roller coaster for him. For a while during the afternoon, when Marc had abandoned his antagonism, Christian thought his troubles were over. He should have known it wouldn't be so easy. The boy was an Alessandro, after all. Maybe not in name, but certainly in personality and stubbornness.

Christian was on the sofa with a cup of coffee at his elbow, deep into an article about a northern Tuscany mudslide that swept away a house, injuring several people, when he heard a pair of voices coming down the stairs toward the salon. His composure took a hit as excitement and anxiety built. This weekend was a significant step toward the rest of his life. What happened here not only determined the future of his country's stability, but also any hope that Christian might have for happiness.

He pushed aside the thought that he didn't deserve Noelle or the joy she brought to his life. He'd lost her once because of his selfish stupidity. Screwing up a second time was not an option.

Christian was on his feet and moving to the stairs as his energetic son brushed past him in a mad dash to get to the dining room and the promised waffles. Chuckling, Christian held his hand out to Noelle as she completed her descent. His pulse bucked as she placed her elegant fingers against his palm and he found his lips curving into a foolish grin.

"Good morning," he said, his voice low and intimate. "You look beautiful."

Today's dress was a half sleeve, French blue sheath, paired with a whimsical pendant necklace. She'd donned flats instead of her usual pumps, which reminded Christian of her petite stature and inspired his protective instincts. Not that she needed his help. Her brown eyes sparkled with confidence above her cheerful smile.

"Thank you." To his surprise, she linked her arm with his as they headed out of the salon. "It was nice of you to send Elise to watch Marc. I was able to shower and dress without any interruption."

She gave a heartfelt sigh that made him long to pull her into a quiet corner and sink his fingers into the dark, wavy hair cascading over her shoulders. The lingering aftermath of the morning's fiery kiss continued to pulse through his veins like a potent cocktail consumed too quickly.

"You're welcome." Despite three cups of strong coffee, he felt sluggish and tongue-tied with her body pressed along his side.

"Will we be going to your winery today? I'm looking forward to seeing where Sherdana's finest vintages are made."

"I've arranged a tour and lunch with pairings of our best wines. Bracci Vineyards and Winery employs a world-class chef, and he's promised to amaze us with his cuisine."

"That sounds wonderful, but what about Marc?"

"My winemaker has several children near Marc's age who are eager to meet him. I assure you he will not be bored."

"Sounds like you have it all figured out."

Christian smiled at her, wishing that was true. His heart and mind were on the same page. He wanted to marry Noelle and make Marc his legitimate son, but instinct told him what might happen for appearance's sake wouldn't bring him the fulfillment he craved. There were those in-between moments when she didn't notice his attention, her smile faded and the sparkle left her eyes. She was putting on a good show for both Marc and him, but Christian sensed she had doubts.

After breakfast Christian spent an hour throwing a ball with Marc in the outer courtyard while Noelle looked on. The boy was crazy about American baseball and had brought a ball and his mitt with him. Christian didn't spend a lot of time in the US, but had several business colleagues he spoke to regularly who had introduced him to the sport. Given his son's fascination with the game, Christian decided he'd better get up to speed quickly.

On the five-mile drive to the winery, Marc rattled on about fastballs and curveballs from the backseat of the blue convertible Maserati Christian kept at the castle. Since the autumn day was sunny and mild, he drove with the top down, his attention split between the empty country road and Noelle's flawless profile as she lifted her face to the sun.

"What a glorious day," she said, stretching her arm across the seat to rake her nails through his hair. "Did you plan this, too?"

Something about her tone made him think she was mocking him. "I ordered it specially for you." He dropped a kiss in her palm. "I only want the best for you."

She withdrew her hand and made a fist as if to capture his kiss. "It's nice to hear."

"You don't believe me." It wasn't a question, but an accusation.

From the backseat, Marc interjected his own question. "When we get there, will I get to stomp grapes?"

Christian's mood brightened at yet another chance to curry favor with his son. "Sure." Although the grape harvest wasn't set to happen for another week, there would likely be a way to pick a few grapes and let Marc and the other kids participate in the ritual.

"No." Noelle shook her head, adamantly opposed.

"Mama, please."

"I think your mother is worried that it will stain your feet purple."

"Will it? That's great."

He shot Noelle a triumphant look, not the least bit daunted by her scowl. Christian intended to do whatever it took to win his son's love. Even if it meant siding with him against his mother from time to time."

"Christian, I don't think that's a great idea."

"It'll be fun. Something he can show off at school and make the other kids jealous."

"Wine-colored feet?" She shook her head in a maternal show of disgust. "Okay, you can stomp grapes."

While Marc whooped in the backseat, Christian reached over and squeezed Noelle's hand in thanks. Her lips softened into a smile at the gesture, and she put her hand atop his.

The car rolled down a long driveway flanked by fields of grapevines and came to rest near the low building that housed the tasting room and an intimate space available for private parties and lunches such as the one Christian had planned today with Noelle.

Almost before Christian turned off the engine, Marc had unbuckled his seat belt and was keyed for the instant his mother opened the passenger door and tipped her seat forward. He wiggled through the door and was off across the lawn in a flash, heading for the tasting-room door. Noelle called after him, but Marc was too excited to slow down. By the time she and Christian reached the building, Marc had disappeared inside.

"I love his enthusiasm," Christian commented as he held the door open for Noelle. "Everything is an adventure. You've done a good job raising him."

"Thank you, but the job's not over yet." She paused in the doorway and touched Christian's arm. "I know I haven't done much to improve your relationship with Marc, but I want you to know that watching you with him this weekend has made me realize how important it is that you two bond." She paused. "No matter what happens between us, I want you and Marc to have as much time together as possible."

"I appreciate that." While he was grateful for her approval, he was less than pleased that she continued to doubt whether they had a future as a family.

"Mama, is this where I get to stomp grapes?" Marc tugged at her hand. "Can I do it now?"

Christian chuckled. "Let me talk to Louis and get it all set up," he told his impatient son. "Why don't you see if Daphne has some fresh grape juice for you to try." He indicated a pretty blonde girl behind the bar. While Marc raced toward the bar and climbed up onto the tall stool, Christian turned to Noelle. "Give me a couple minutes to get Marc settled. Then we can go on our tour."

# Nine

Noelle waited until Christian disappeared through a door in the back of the tasting room before joining her son. Even without a single sip of wine, she was suffering the effects of intoxication. Not that she could be blamed for feeling giddy and light-headed when Christian turned on the charm. The man had convinced her to let her son stomp grapes. Noelle shook her head, contemplating the reactions of Marc's teachers and his classmates' parents after he broadcast his weekend's activities at school. No doubt she would have some explaining to do.

But to see her son so happy was worth it. Noelle sighed. Watching Marc's wariness toward his father fade made her question her decision to not tell Christian that she was pregnant. At the time she'd been afraid he'd reject her again. No. That wasn't the whole truth. She'd also been angry.

She was still angry.

Last night she hadn't gone to Christian's room motivated solely by desire. She'd had something to prove to herself and to him. She needed to prove that she could surrender her body to the passion he aroused without giving over her heart at the same time. Leaving as abruptly as she had was meant to demonstrate that this time around she wasn't going to lead with her heart but her head. The woman she was today never would have taken the little Christian had offered her five years earlier.

But she would never be truly happy keeping her emotions bottled up, either. There had to be a happy medium between giving too much and not giving enough.

At Marc's insistence, she sat beside him and tasted his grape juice, pronouncing it delicious. He gave her a huge grin and then went back to telling Daphne all about the armor he'd seen at Bracci Castle. Noelle ran her fingers through his thick, dark hair and considered how many times a day he reminded her of Christian.

As if summoned by her thoughts, he appeared at her side. "Ready for the tour? Louis's son is going to take Marc to where the other children are. They'll play for a while and have lunch. Afterward Louis is going to set up the grape-stomp contest to see who is the best stomper."

"Me!" Marc exclaimed, jumping down from his stool, fists in the air.

Noelle laughed at his enthusiasm. "Well, you certainly have the energy for it." She ruffled his hair and watched him run toward a tall boy who was gesturing for him to follow.

Half an hour later, she and Christian came to the end of the tour, and Noelle was eager to sample some of the wines she'd learned about. "I'll never take wine for granted ever again," she promised Christian before thanking their guide, Bracci Vineyard and Winery's exceptional wine-maker, Louis Beauchon.

"I'm glad to hear it." Louis was a handsome man in his early forties with prematurely gray hair and striking blue eyes. He had a ready smile and an abundance of hilarious stories about people he'd worked with during his twenty-five years of winemaking. "You'll have to let me know what you think of our wines after lunch."

"I'm afraid my palate is nowhere near as experienced as Prince Christian's, but I look forward to sharing my impressions."

"That's all I need. I'll see you later at the grape stomp."

Christian steered her along a curving path that wound through the garden at the back of the tasting room and through a set of French doors that led into an intimate dining room. At the center of the space was a single table set for two and covered with a white tablecloth and fine china. Two servers, dressed in black and white, stood to one side of the room, welcoming smiles on their faces.

Once Christian had assisted her into her seat and joined her at the table, the servers stepped forward and poured the first wine. Noelle lost herself in Christian's deep voice as he described the wine being served and commented on the meal to come. One course followed another, each being served with a different wine. Despite the small portions, Noelle was beginning to feel overcome by all the rich, flavorful dishes by the time dessert arrived.

"Chef Cheval is a genius, but I don't think I could eat another bite," she protested, as a delicate chocolate basket filled with white chocolate mousse and a single raspberry was placed before her. As with each course, the gorgeous plating made the food irresistible. How could she resist dessert? "Maybe just a bite."

Noelle didn't notice Christian's intense regard until

she'd scraped the plate clean and set her spoon aside. She cocked her head at him but had no opportunity to ask why he was staring. A short, round man in chef's whites entered the room, his toque set at a jaunty angle.

"Prince Christian!" the man exclaimed in a deep baritone. "How wonderful to have you back."

"Chef Cheval." Christian gestured in Noelle's direction. "This is Noelle Dubone."

"Chef, this was the most amazing meal I've ever had. Thank you."

The chef bowed to her. "I'm so glad you enjoyed it. Prince Christian said I must prepare only the best for you."

"He did?" She shot Christian a wry look, wondering how many other women had been given such royal treatment. "Well, you've both made my visit to Bracci memorable."

"You will come back? I appreciate a woman who likes to eat."

Noelle laughed. "Of course," she said, growing more and more accustomed to the idea of becoming a permanent fixture in Christian's life. "I appreciate a man who cooks with your flair."

"Well, good." The chef gave Christian an audacious wink before taking his leave.

The servers cleared the dessert plates and topped off both water and wineglasses before taking their leave. Noelle swirled her wine, soothed by the excellent food, the early fall scents and the distant sound of children at play. Relaxed to the point of sleepiness, she wondered if there might be time for a nap when they returned to Christian's castle.

"Did you mean what you said about coming back?" Christian's abrupt question cut through her lethargy.

"I did." She stumbled a little over the words, wondering why he'd grown so serious. "Why?"

"I didn't want to pressure you this weekend by talking about the future, but after last night, I think I have a right to ask about your intentions."

"My intentions?" Noelle wondered when the world had turned upside down. "Since when does a man ask a woman about her intentions regarding their relationship?"

"Since the man has stated his desire to marry the woman, and she comes to his room with seduction on her mind and leaves the man feeling as if he's been nothing more than her plaything."

Noelle pressed her lips together to hide a smile, but couldn't stop her eyes from dancing. Christian growled at her in mock severity.

She replied with an equally insincere apology. "I didn't mean to take you or your body for granted. As for my intentions, I plan to continue as I did last evening, exploring our mutual chemistry and seeing where things lead."

To her surprise Christian sat back and crossed his arms over his chest. "Not good enough."

"No?"

"I'm serious about you. This isn't going to be a casual affair where we play it by ear or take it one day at a time."

"Because your family is pressuring you to marry and produce an heir who can rule one day." Noelle tensed at the unwelcome reminder of why she and Marc were here this weekend. "I'm not going to decide the rest of my life or Marc's in a few short days no matter how wonderful they've been. I need time to decide what's right for him."

"And you're not yet sure I am?"

"It's not about you. It's the responsibility he'll face one day. You once told me how Gabriel changed when he realized he was destined to be king. I don't know if I want that for Marc."

Christian reached across the table and took her hand in his. "With my father in perfect health and Gabriel so young, Marc will be more than ready when the time comes for him to rule."

While Noelle appreciated Christian's logic, she wasn't ready to lose her baby to the country of Sherdana. "I just wish he was old enough to help me with this decision."

"Mama." Marc skidded through the doorway, flushed and disheveled. "We're going to stomp grapes. Come on." Without waiting for her, he ran back out of the room.

Laughing, she got to her feet. "You heard your son," she said, tugging on Christian's hand. "Let's go."

"He certainly has the imperious demeanor of a future monarch." Grinning, Christian threw his napkin onto the table and stood.

"Don't you mean tyrant?"

"He must get his bossy nature from his mother." Christian's arm snaked around her waist before she reached the French doors. "I find that an unexpected turn on."

He spun her into his arms and captured her lips in a sizzling kiss. Noelle sagged against him, admiring his knack for turning a lighthearted jab into a sincere compliment. Even knowing they could be caught at any second, Noelle darted out her tongue to taste the smooth chocolate and heady wine lingering on Christian's lips. His fingers tightened almost painfully against her ribs before he pushed her to arm's length.

"You are bad for my willpower," he told her, his voice a husky rasp. "First this morning and now…"

"Mama, are you coming?" Marc's plaintive wail came from across the yard.

Noelle gathered a shaky breath. "If we hold up the grape stomp much longer, my son will never forgive me."

Hand in hand they walked around the corner of the building where the bulk of the wine process happened and came upon a gathering of children and workers. Although the official start to the harvest was a week away, enough grapes had been gathered to fill three half wine barrels for the children to stomp.

In addition to Marc, Louis's youngest son and the vineyard manager's daughter were barefoot and ready to begin. The half casks had been set on a platform. Below each stomping container sat collecting jars for the juice. The children would pulverize the grapes with their feet, and the first one to produce the required amount of liquid would win. Seeing her son's grim determination, she knew Marc would give it his all.

"He has my competitive spirit," Christian murmured near her ear a second before Louis's wife signaled the start of the contest.

Noelle relaxed against the arm Christian slipped around her waist, enjoying his solidness against her back. "Yes. Some days that gets to be a problem."

Despite her words, she rooted for her son. Not that Marc needed the encouragement. Displaying the abundant energy that exhausted both Noelle and her mother on a daily basis, he ran in place, his concentration riveted on the grapes beneath his feet. Watching him, Noelle realized that while he was her baby and she wanted to protect him from harm, Marc was more resilient than she gave him credit for. He wouldn't suffer beneath the extreme media attention on the horizon. Nor would he be pushed into uncomfortable circumstances by Christian's family. There was too much of his father in him for him to take on the weight of rule until he was damn good and ready. And she hoped he had enough of her common sense to know when that moment was.

Beside her, Christian cheered as Marc was the first to accumulate the requisite amount of juice. After planting a firm, enthusiastic kiss on her cheek, Christian strode to the platform and swung his triumphant son out of the half cask. Noelle winced as vivid purple juice dripped from her son's feet and stained Christian's khaki pants. Heedless of the damage to his clothes, Christian set Marc on his hip and each threw a celebratory fist in the air.

Noelle felt the tiniest prick of sadness. Where once she'd been everything to Marc, she recognized that his father would soon be occupying more and more of his attention. Noelle couldn't help the panic that welled up. She'd built such a comfortable, safe life for herself and Marc, but so many changes were looming on the horizon.

Louis's wife came to her side. "Try lemon juice to get the grape stains off his feet."

"That works?"

The woman grinned. "It will help."

While Noelle chatted with Louis's wife, Christian cleaned off Marc's feet and wrangled him back into his socks and shoes. Hand in hand they then walked in her direction.

"Did you see how good I stomped, Mama?" Marc ran in place, demonstrating his winning technique. He gripped a bottle of sparkling grape juice, his prize for winning.

"I did." She noticed Marc hadn't released Christian's hand. Her chest tightened, but she offered her son a proud smile. "You are the best grape stomper in all Sherdana."

"He certainly is," Christian said, his gaze fond as it rested on Marc. "Are you ready to head back to the castle?"

"I think I've had enough excitement for one day. And someone needs a bath." She gazed pointedly at her son's feet.

"No, Mama. I want to show everyone at school that I stomped grapes."

"You can tell them about it," Noelle countered.

To her surprise, Marc didn't argue further. Instead, he waved goodbye to his new friends and trotted ahead of his parents to the lot where Christian's car waited.

On the way back to Bracci Castle, Marc's excited chatter gave way to silence.

Christian glanced over his shoulder. "He's out."

"Not surprising." Noelle felt a yawn coming on. The slow country pace combined with the delicious, filling lunch was making her sleepy. "I guess his bath will have to wait until later."

"I could use a nap myself," Christian said. "I didn't get a lot of sleep last night."

Noelle ignored the pointed look he shot her way. "That's odd. You were in bed by eleven."

"Yes, but I had a very eventful evening and couldn't figure out why it came to such an abrupt end."

"Perhaps because it wouldn't do for the eventfulness to become common knowledge."

"Why not when it's only a matter of time before we make our relationship official?"

"You seem very sure that's how things will go."

"I'm not so much confident as determined. Now that Marc is getting more accustomed to me, I expect to spend a lot more time with him. Which means you'll also be seeing more of me. You can't resist me forever."

Noelle sighed. Truth was, she couldn't resist him at all.

Christian slid into a charcoal-gray suit coat and straightened his blue-gray tie. The full-length mirror in his Carone apartment dressing room reflected back a somber aristocrat with chiseled features and wary eyes. It was not the face of a man about to propose to the mother of his son.

Since returning from the weekend at Bracci Castle five days ago, Christian had spent every evening with Noelle and Marc. They'd dined at her farmhouse, the palace and the restaurant that served American burgers. Tonight, however, he'd arranged for a private yacht to take Noelle and him on a romantic cruise down the river. During dinner, he planned to officially ask her to be his wife. On his nightstand sat the five-carat princess-cut diamond she would be wearing three hours from now.

As his driver wove through Carone's streets on the way out of the city, Christian reflected that he wasn't giving Noelle the time she'd asked for to decide if this was the right future for her and Marc. Last weekend it had been easy to promise her space. They'd reconnected both physically and emotionally. But these past five days had been hell.

He wanted to wake up with Noelle and have breakfast with Marc. To throw the ball with his son in the evenings and read him a bedtime story before taking Noelle in his arms and spending the night making love to her. A chaste good-night kiss at eight o'clock was completely unsatisfying.

When the car stopped in Noelle's driveway, Christian didn't wait for the driver to open his door. He was impatient to see Noelle and get their evening started. Before he could knock, Noelle's front door whipped open and Marc grinned at him from the foyer.

"Mama," he called, whirling on stocking feet and racing back into the house. "Prince Papa is here."

The blending of his two titles continued to amuse Christian. He suspected that the "prince" half would eventually go away. Until then, he was satisfied that his son had accepted Christian's role in his life.

"Marc, I'm right here," his mother admonished as she emerged from the main living room. "There's no reason to shout."

Christian stepped into the house and shut the door behind him. Word was out that he and Noelle had been spending time together, and he didn't want any telescopic lenses capturing the kiss he was about to give her.

Tonight's dress was a retro-style teal silk with a matching long-sleeve coat. The hemline was a bit shorter than usual and displayed a tantalizing amount of shapely leg. She wore her hair in an elegant topknot that he couldn't wait to dishevel. Simple pearls adorned her delicate earlobes, and a matching strand encircled her neck. She gave him a welcoming smile, and he stepped forward to draw her firmly into his embrace.

The warm feminine scent of her made his head spin as he claimed her mouth in a tender, poignant kiss. He kept a ruthless hold on his libido. This was not the time nor the place to show her how five days of abstinence had driven him mad with longing. They had all evening and much of the night for him to demonstrate how fully beneath her spell he'd fallen.

"Shall we go?" he purred beside her ear, feeling the shiver that passed through her muscles. "I have a full night planned."

She pulled back and regarded him with alarm. "I can't stay out all night. Marc gets up early and will expect me to be here."

"I will have you back before the roosters start to crow." For most people this would only be a saying, but in fact Noelle kept several chickens on her acre of land, and Marc had mentioned the rooster's predawn bugling several times.

"Thank you."

Christian held her hand as the town car wove through Carone to where the yacht was moored. Earlier that day, he'd prepared a speech. It ran through his mind like a hamster on a wheel and he found himself oddly tongue-tied. Thankfully, Noelle had never been bothered by silence between them, but tonight her tranquil acceptance offered him no solace.

After boarding the yacht, Christian led her to the salon. The September warm spell would enable them to enjoy a romantic dinner on deck where they could observe the lights of the city reflecting off the water as dusk became night. But that would come later. He had something he needed to get out of the way first.

A bottle of champagne was chilling in a silver bucket on the bar. Two tall flutes stood beside it, waiting to be filled. Christian had asked for privacy during this cruise except while dinner was being served. He wanted no audience this evening. Since the champagne had been opened, all Christian had to do was pour the sparkling liquid and hand Noelle a glass. He was happy to see that his hands didn't shake as he clinked his flute with hers.

"To us." He felt rather than heard his voice break awkwardly and swallowed far too much of the fizzy wine. The bubbles burned as they went down, and he coughed.

Noelle peered at him over her flute and cleared her own throat. "I think we should get married."

A racing speedboat passed recklessly close to the yacht, almost drowning out her words. Wondering if he'd heard her properly, Christian searched Noelle's expression.

"Did you say we should get married?" The noise of the speedboat was receding, but Christian continued to hear buzzing.

"Why do you sound so surprised? I thought that's what

you wanted." Anxiety flitted across her delicate features. "Have you changed your mind?"

"No." Explaining to her that he'd planned out the romantic evening with the sole intent of proposing seemed a little anticlimactic. "You've just caught me by surprise."

"I said I needed some time to think about it." Her gaze was fixed on the passing shore. "After watching you with Marc this week, I realized just how much he's missed not having his father in his life."

"So, this is about Marc and me." He'd been thinking in terms of finding the sort of marital bliss and perfect little family that Gabriel and Olivia enjoyed with the twins.

"Well, yes. Isn't that what you've wanted all along? To become Marc's father and to legitimize him as your heir?" Her obvious confusion proved she had no clue how his feelings for her had grown over the past couple of weeks.

And now he had no reason to tell her. She was happy with her decision to marry him. They would have a good partnership, and the sex between them was fantastic. Why muddy things with sentimental declarations of romantic love?

"It's exactly what I want," he told her, pulling the small jewelry box out of his pocket and opening the lid so she could see the ring. "And I've had this waiting for the moment you agreed."

Christian was happy to let her think he hadn't planned for anything out of the ordinary tonight. He lifted her left hand and slipped the ring onto her finger. As eager as he'd been all day to present this token of his commitment, the way the moment had played out left him with a hollow feeling in his gut.

"It's beautiful," she breathed, sounding more emotional than she had while suggesting they get married. She lifted onto her tiptoes and kissed him.

For once desire didn't consume him at the slightest brush of her lips. He tasted the champagne she'd sipped and inwardly grimaced at the bitterness of his disappointment. Calling himself every sort of fool, Christian plunged his tongue into her mouth and feasted on her surrender. She was his. That was all that mattered.

"We should tell my family tomorrow," he said, sweeping kisses across her forehead. He drew back and gave her his best smile.

"Marc first," she replied. "I don't want him hearing it from someone at school. Can you come by in the morning?"

"Of course."

They carried their champagne outside and sat at the beautifully set table. Around them white lights had been strung to provide a romantic atmosphere. Servers brought the first course and, by mutual agreement, Christian and Noelle spoke no more about their plans for the future until they could be safely alone again.

"The timing on this is quite good," Christian said. "Ariana returned from Paris yesterday, and Nic and Brooke aren't set to leave for Los Angeles until the end of the week. We can tell my whole family at once."

"That's wonderful news. Have you thought when you'd like the wedding to take place?"

"We could elope to Ithaca the way Gabriel and Olivia did."

Noelle shook her head. "I don't think your mother would approve. Perhaps we could have a Christmas wedding?"

He didn't like the idea of waiting three months to make her his wife, but having been on the sidelines for his brothers' weddings, he understood a great deal went into organizing a royal affair.

"Whatever you desire."

She gave him a funny little smile. "Just don't bother you with any of the details?"

"I'm sure between you, Olivia and my mother, any opinion I might have would be shot down in an instant."

The large diamond on her left hand winked at him as she lifted the champagne flute to her lips. "I promise you can have a voice in the arrangements if you tell me the one thing you always pictured having at your wedding."

"I never imagined getting married." Christian saw no reason to avoid the truth.

"No, I suppose you didn't."

Her smile wasn't as bright as some he'd seen, and he felt compelled to change that.

"It took the right woman to change my mind."

"The right circumstances."

Christian wanted to argue. To convince her that he had other reasons for marrying her besides legitimizing Marc and securing the throne for his family. Five years ago, knowing she'd never choose success over love, he'd manipulated the circumstances that swept her out of his life. She'd never believe he did it for her own good. Or that his actions had been noble even if on the surface they appeared selfish.

So, instead of creating conflict on the heels of a great victory, he did what any sane man would. He said to hell with dinner, took her in his arms and carried her to the master cabin.

Noelle rolled onto her side in the yacht's roomy master bedroom to watch the play of muscles in Christian's back and the delectable curve of his bare butt as he crossed the cabin to open a window and let in some cool evening air.

"The crew is going to wonder what happened to us,"

Noelle commented, her breath catching as Christian turned in her direction and shot her a wicked grin.

From his lustrous mahogany hair to his absurdly long toes and every magnificent line, dip and rise in between, he was hers. The jubilant thought lightened her heart and weighed on her mind.

"You don't think they heard us and know exactly what we're up to?"

Fresh air spilled across her overheated flesh and she broke out in goose bumps. She should feel embarrassed that her impassioned cries and his climactic shouts had penetrated the stateroom's thin walls. Instead, she found herself grinning.

"Too bad we didn't open the window beforehand. We could have given the entire riverbank something to talk about tomorrow."

Christian dropped onto the mattress and reached for her. "We could go for an encore."

Laughing, Noelle batted his hands away from her breast and thigh before snuggling against his left side and dropping her head onto his chest. His fingers traced soothing patterns on her hip as they lay together in silence.

It was hard to be this close to such a superb example of masculinity and not let herself go exploring. He sighed as she traced his collarbone and worked her way across his pectoral muscles. Glancing at his face, she noted his thick lashes lying against his cheeks. This gave her the chance to survey the right side of his upper body, where the worst of the scars were gathered. Moving with care, she grazed the tips of her fingers over the damaged flesh. Christian flinched.

She jerked her hand away. "Did I hurt you?"

"No." His chest expanded as he sucked in a ragged

breath. He stared at the ceiling, gold eyes dull. "The scars are ugly." His voice rang with self-disgust.

Noelle doubted many people saw this darker side of Christian. In public he exuded capability and confidence that she knew took a great deal of energy to maintain. Only with those he truly trusted could he let down his guard. Noelle had been happy to lend him what strength she could.

"You got them rescuing Talia after Andre lost control of his car," she reminded him. "They're your badge of courage."

"You know what happened?" His muscles tensed. "How? That was never public knowledge."

"You forget that I spent a great deal of time with Olivia in the days leading up to her wedding. For some reason she wanted to impress upon me what a brave, honorable man you were." Noelle suspected the princess had known Marc was Christian's son for some time. She kissed his damaged shoulder and felt a shudder rage through his body. "I don't understand why you kept the truth about the accident a secret. You were a hero."

He shook his head. "I blame myself for the crash. If I hadn't been chasing after Andre's car, he never would have driven so recklessly and lost control."

He'd raced into the night after Talia, his ex-lover, abandoning Noelle at a party to do so. Getting ready for the party that night, slipping on the bracelet Christian had given her for her birthday, she'd been giddy with anticipation of their first public appearance as a couple. But after that night, it was a long, long time before she was happy again.

Noelle wasn't sure why she'd picked the evening of her engagement to dredge up the past. Maybe her subconscious wanted to remind her that Christian held too much power over her happiness. Message received. This was going to be a marriage built on respect and passion. Friendship and sex. No reason she needed to yield her heart and risk being hurt again.

Christian's long fingers swept into her hair as he brought his lips to hers for a long, searing kiss. Noelle melted beneath his hot mouth and caressing hands. As her blood raced through her veins and pooled in her loins, she smiled. Her body she could give him without reservation.

She would be his wife, his princess and the mother of his children. Noelle hoped it would be enough.

# Ten

Noelle sat on her office sofa, her bare feet tucked beneath her, and tapped her pencil against the sketchbook on her lap. The enormous diamond on her left hand felt awkward and strange. She caught herself staring at it a dozen times in the past hour as her mind struggled to assimilate the dramatic changes taking place. She was engaged to a prince. And not just any prince, but the prince of her dreams. It didn't seem possible.

Of course, it wasn't a fairy-tale engagement. Last night she'd been the one to suggest that they marry. She had merely formalized what Christian had already proposed, but it wasn't as if he'd dropped to one knee and pledged his undying love. At least he'd been ready with a ring.

She spun the diamond so it wasn't visible and turned her attention back to the sketchbook. To no avail. In two hours she and Christian would be breaking the news to his family. She'd already told her mother, but Marc didn't yet know. He'd woken before dawn with a stomachache and she'd kept him home from school. With him sick it hadn't seemed the best time to divulge that she and Christian were getting married, despite the fact that he and his father were getting along very well these days.

Her cell phone buzzed, and Noelle abandoned her work with a relieved sigh. The number on the screen caused a spike in her pulse. She sat up straight and slipped her shoes back on.

"Noelle Dubone," she said in a crisp voice, wondering if it was good or bad news to hear back so soon on a business venture.

"Noelle, it's Victor. I hope I'm reaching you at a good time."

"Yes. Fine." She sounded a trifle breathless and told herself to calm down. "How are you?"

"Good. Good. I'm calling to let you know that I just spoke with Jim Shae, and he is very interested in backing you with a ready-to-wear line of bridal fashions here in the States."

Victor Chamberlain was a friend of Geoff's who she'd met in London several years ago. An American businessman whose daughter had been looking for something fresh and unique in a wedding dress, he'd become Noelle's first big client. Last February during New York Fashion Week, he'd introduced her to several venture capitalists and suggested she should consider expanding into ready-to-wear.

Creating one-of-a kind wedding dresses was vastly different from mass-producing an entire collection, so she'd teamed up with Victor to create a business plan that he'd pitched to investors.

"That's wonderful news." With joy dancing across her nerve endings, it took a few seconds for reality to strike. What was she thinking? She was engaged to a Sherdanian prince and needed to start planning now in order to make a royal wedding happen by Christmas. Keeping up with her current clients would be stressful enough. She didn't have time to start a new business venture.

"Can you be in New York next week? Jim would like to meet with you and discuss details."

Next week? Noelle worried her lower lip as she went to check her schedule. "How many days would I need to be there?"

Victor hesitated before answering. "At least three. Besides Jim, I want to set up meetings with buyers from the top bridal shops and media interviews. You should start planning for New York Fashion Week in February. You'll need a terrific venue. I know someone who can help with that."

"Three days…" Noelle's mind worked furiously.

Perhaps she and Christian should postpone the announcement of their engagement until after her New York trip. With a start she realized there was no question in her mind that she intended to embark on this business venture. Was splitting her attention between Sherdana and New York a wise move at the beginning of her marriage? On the other hand, did Christian plan to stop all business travel? Not likely.

"Let me know as soon as possible when you'll be flying in," Victor continued.

"I'll make all my arrangements and be in touch later today."

First of all, she needed to tell Christian what had just happened. But as she scrolled through her contacts for his number, she faltered. How would he view her decision to jump into a major business venture without talking to him about it first? He should be happy for her. But would he question her priorities? Her commitment to this marriage?

Or was she the one questioning her commitment?

Noelle sank into her office chair and stared out the window overlooking the alley behind her salon. In two hours she would be announcing her intention to marry Christian. She spun the ring on her finger. Once word got out, she'd better be ready to go forward. Not only would a broken engagement create a scandal the country didn't need, but her actions would confuse Marc and set a bad example for him.

Conflict churned Noelle's insides. Christian deserved to be a full-time father to Marc, and that would be better accomplished if Noelle honored her engagement and married Christian. Marc benefited. Christian benefited. The country benefited. Three wins. Noelle didn't have to feel guilty about focusing on her business instead of playing the part of dutiful wife. Christian was getting the heir he wanted.

Despite arriving at a reasonable conclusion, Noelle wasn't convinced Christian would agree. She keyed his number and heard the call going through.

"Noelle." He purred in her ear. "I was just thinking about you."

Her toes curled in her pink, superfine Louboutin stilettos. With his warm brandy voice flowing from the phone's speaker, she was hard-pressed to summon all her earlier doubts. Of course, she wanted to marry Christian. No other man could make her come alive just by breathing her name.

"I've been thinking about you, as well." Was that her coming across all sexy and mysterious? She curved her body sideways in the chair, any trace of the capable businesswoman lost beneath a rush of feminine pleasure at hearing her lover's voice.

"I'm heading into a conference call in a moment. Is everything okay with Marc?"

Suddenly Noelle couldn't find the words to share her

confusion and doubts. "He's better. Turns out it wasn't the flu but an entire bag of cookies that caused his stomachache. I just wondered if you wanted to have dinner at my house tonight."

"Absolutely. If you think Marc will be well enough, we can tell him about our engagement."

"That's what I planned. The sooner the better." And she would also tell him about her new venture. Together they would figure out the best way forward.

"I have back-to-back meetings between now and when I'm supposed to pick you up for our meeting with my family, and I don't want to be late so I've arranged for a car to take you to the palace."

"That's not necessary. I've made my own way to the palace a dozen times. I'll be fine."

"It's what I want. You are no longer visiting as a designer or a guest."

Hearing his determination, Noelle conceded. "Very well. Just don't leave me facing your family alone."

"Never fear." Rich amusement filled his tone. "I'll see you at three."

Noelle disconnected the call and sat with the phone in her lap, preparing herself to do the right thing for all concerned.

Christian stared at the slow-moving traffic ahead of him, about to break the promise he'd made to Noelle two hours earlier. He had ten minutes to get to the palace and fifteen minutes of driving ahead of him. He should have anticipated that his meeting with Gaston would run late. The man was a savvy politician in the perfect position to block Christian from securing land he needed outside Carone to develop his next project. The negotiations had been difficult.

With Sherdana's economic troubles easing thanks to an influx of technology businesses, Christian had decided to focus more of his attention on investing close to home. This would mean less travel and more time spent with Noelle and Marc. It was important as a new husband and father to put his family first.

Drumming his thumbs against the steering wheel, Christian willed the cars in front of him to move. His impatience wasn't just about the traffic. He was eager to see Noelle again. Having to postpone telling Marc this morning had been disappointing, but sharing their news with his family was the next best thing.

When Christian arrived in the family's private living room, Noelle was already there with his parents, Nic, Brooke and Ariana. Standing at ease beside his sister, Noelle looked stunning in a richly embroidered pale pink coat over a simple ivory dress. Before making his way to Noelle's side, Christian swung by to greet his parents.

"You're late," the king scolded.

"Traffic," Christian explained. "Besides, Gabriel and Olivia aren't here yet."

The queen offered her cheek for his kiss. "You'd better have good news for us."

"The best." He smiled his most confident grin.

Obligations satisfied, he headed toward Noelle. As he took his place beside her, Gabriel and Olivia rushed hand-in-hand into the room. Their exuberant smiles drew everyone's attention. Christian experienced an uncomfortable stab of envy at the strength of their connection. They were surrounded by family and yet so in tune with each other. Would he and Noelle ever get to a point where they enjoyed that sort of intimacy?

"We have wonderful news," Gabriel began, his unrestrained delight making him seem far younger than thirty. "We are going to be parents."

For a moment the room was deathly quiet as Christian's family absorbed this impossible announcement. Olivia had undergone a hysterectomy four months earlier, rendering her incapable of having children.

The queen was the first to recover her voice. "How?"

"My eggs were viable for a month after my operations. The doctors were able to harvest several. We found a surrogate and just came from her first doctor's appointment. Everything looks good." Olivia turned a radiant smile on Gabriel.

He bent his head and gave her a quick kiss. Then he glanced around the room. "And we're having twins."

Ariana ran to Olivia and threw her arms around her sister-in-law. Nic and Brooke stepped up next. While a part of Christian was thrilled for his older brother, most of him was numb. He glanced at Noelle to gauge her reaction. She watched the happy couple through eyes that shone brightly with tears. Christian felt his throat lock up and could only stare, mind blank, as his parents stepped up for their turn to congratulate their son and daughter-in-law.

Noelle poked him in the ribs and whispered, "Go congratulate them. This is amazing news."

"What about our news?" He sounded like a grumpy old man. "It's pretty amazing, too."

"This is their moment. I don't want to ruin it." She placed the flat of her hand against his back and gave him a shove. While she didn't have the strength to move him, her recommendation was clear.

Was there some other reason why she didn't want to announce their engagement? Was she thinking of backing out now that Gabriel and Olivia had figured out a way to supply an heir for the throne?

Christian pushed aside concern and caught Noelle's hand in his. Together they joined the circle of well-wishers.

"You seem to have a knack for producing twins," Christian told his brother, smiling despite his heavy heart.

"At least these two won't be identical," Gabriel replied.

Several members of the staff brought the champagne that Christian had made sure was on ice to toast his engagement, and everyone except Brooke—who was pregnant—enjoyed a glass. No one seemed to recall that Christian had organized the family meeting or wonder what his announcement might have been.

The frustration he'd begun feeling the instant Noelle suggested they put off sharing the news of their engagement began to grow. He'd put all his energy into convincing Noelle that they belonged together as a family and now his brother had to come along at the absolute moment that Christian was the happiest he'd ever been and spoil everything.

Thirty minutes into the celebration, he pulled her aside. "I really think we should announce our engagement."

Noelle glanced at Gabriel and Olivia. "Now isn't a good time. And I need to get back to my shop."

His dismay expanded. "I thought we'd have the afternoon to celebrate making our engagement official."

"Something came up earlier that I need to take care of."

Considering that he'd arrived at the palace almost twenty minutes late because of his own meeting schedule, Christian forced down his irritation.

"What time should I come by tonight?"

She pressed her lips together and didn't meet his eyes. "About that. Why don't we wait a little while before we tell Marc."

"Why don't I take you back to your shop, and we can discuss that on the way there."

"Christian—"

"You owe me an explanation for your sudden turn-around."

She ducked her head and nodded. "I know."

Without drawing attention to themselves, they slipped out of the room and headed to the side entrance nearest the family quarters where Christian had left his car.

After assisting Noelle into the passenger seat, he slipped behind the wheel and started the powerful engine. Wasting no time on preliminaries, he stomped on the gas and, as the car shot forward, demanded, "What's going on?"

"Gabriel and Olivia are going to be parents. This changes everything."

It did, and he hated them for it. "It changes nothing. I'm still Marc's father. I deserve to be in his life."

"Of course you do, but now we don't need to rush into anything." Both her words and her tone betrayed her relief.

Christian ground his teeth together, using only half his attention to negotiate past slower-moving vehicles. "I didn't realize we were rushing."

"Didn't you? We were planning for a Christmas wedding." She was spinning her engagement ring around and around. "You wanted to make Marc your legal heir as soon as possible so that your family would continue to enjoy political stability."

"I want to be a family with you and Marc," he corrected.

"And we still can, but it's nothing that has to happen right away."

The problem with her argument was that each day Christian grew more impatient to live under the same roof as her and Marc. His bachelor lifestyle no longer interested him.

"My brother has already demonstrated that he only

knows how to produce girls," Christian argued. "What makes you think this time will be different?"

"In a month or so they'll be able to tell the sex of the babies. In the meantime…" Noelle slipped the ring from her finger and held it out to Christian.

"You're breaking off our engagement already." A statement, not a question.

His heartbeat slowed to a near standstill. This couldn't be happening to him.

"It isn't a real engagement." Clearly her perception of their relationship differed from his. "I mean, we aren't in love or anything, so it's just an arrangement."

She wasn't wrong. He'd used legitimizing their son as an excuse for marriage. As always, taking what appeared to be the easiest path had led him into a bramble hedge. Now he was stuck with the consequences.

"I care about you. I don't want to lose you."

She smiled. "And I care about you, but as you often used to remind me, you aren't cut out for marriage. You were marrying me out of duty. Now you don't have to."

"Keep the ring." He tightened his grip on the steering wheel. "We'll postpone announcing our engagement for a month."

Noelle closed her fist around the diamond and set both hands in her lap. "I don't feel right keeping it."

"It's yours. I bought it for you." He didn't want the damned thing back. "We'll proceed as we've been for a few weeks longer. You're right that we rushed. Circumstances pushed us too fast. Now we have all the time in the world."

When she didn't respond, he glanced over at her. His stomach twisted at her obvious discomfort.

"What?" he prompted.

"See, the thing is…" She hesitated, and stared out the passenger window for so long he thought she might have forgotten he was beside her. "I called you earlier today to tell you about something that just came up."

He did not like the sound of this. "What sort of something?"

"A business opportunity. I have a meeting with an investor next week. He's interested in backing a line of ready-to-wear bridal gowns."

"That's fantastic."

She smiled at his enthusiasm. "I'm very excited."

"You don't seem to be."

"It's just that the potential investor wants me to expand my business in the US, specifically New York City. That's where my meetings are next week."

He was starting to see why she was so subdued. "That's a long commute."

"I was worried about it."

"And now you're not?"

"I think Gabriel and Olivia's news might have allowed us to dodge a bullet."

"How so?"

"You didn't really want to get married, and now you don't have to. Marc is your son. As he gets a little older, we can figure out a visitation schedule that enables you to see as much of him as makes sense."

"And in the meantime?" Christian was having a hard time keeping his rising anger out of his tone. "Am I supposed to just let you take Marc to New York and not see my son?"

"No, of course not. I'll have to travel back and forth between New York and Europe. I have many clients on this side of the Atlantic whom I can't afford to neglect. But I'll be creating a collection to show at New York Fashion Week in February that will kick off my ready-to-wear line and

I'll probably be spending the bulk of my time in America leading up to it."

"Marc should stay here with me." It's not what Christian had intended to suggest. He couldn't imagine living without Noelle or his son, but once again he'd used Marc as a decoy to distract her from the full scope of his emotions.

"I can't leave him in Sherdana. I'm all he's known his whole life. He's too young to understand why his mother is leaving him."

"You don't take him with you every time you travel for business. We'll start small. How long are you going to be in New York next week?"

"A few days."

"That's perfect."

"No."

"You go to New York and meet with your investor while I stay here and take care of Marc. If we'd gotten married, it's what would have eventually happened. The only difference is the lack of a legal document."

She gave a soft gasp. "A custody agreement?"

"A marriage license." Christian stopped the car in front of Noelle's shop and put it in Park. Turning in his seat, he took her hand that held the ring and opened her fingers. "I'm not giving up on the idea of marrying you," he said, slipping the diamond onto her right hand. "Take this ring as a sign of my faith in us as a couple and as a family."

"I'll wear it until I return from New York. At that point we will sit down and discuss what's best for Marc and for you and me."

Which meant he had a little more than a week to convince her to go forward with their plans to get married. If he hoped to convince her they belonged together, he'd better pull out all the stops. He wasn't going to make the mistake of letting her go a second time.

* * *

The morning she was scheduled to leave for New York, Noelle woke with her stomach twisted into knots. She was about to embark on the most ambitious project of her career. To fail would mean she'd not only risked damaging her reputation as a designer and a businesswoman, but had created a rift between Christian and her for nothing.

She'd decided not to leave Marc at home with either his father or her mother. This wasn't a two-day hop to Paris or Milan. This was a ten-hour plane ride and an ocean between them. Her son didn't share her anxiety about their separation. Taking him with her meant Marc would be missing a field trip to the zoo. He'd protested vehemently, and reminding him that they'd visited less than a month ago had only made things worse.

"Marc, please go upstairs and brush your teeth. You must get dressed. The car will be here any moment to take us to the airport." She turned to her mother. "Why is he being like this?"

"He doesn't want to go. Why don't you leave him with me? He shouldn't be stuck in a hotel room in New York while you're working."

While a part of Noelle knew her mother was right, she couldn't quell her uneasiness at the thought of leaving him behind. She'd made arrangements for a nanny to stay with Marc while she conducted business, but didn't know if she was comfortable letting the woman roam around the city alone with him.

A knock sounded on the door. The car she'd arranged to take her and Marc to the airport had finally arrived.

"Marc, the car is here. There is no more time for games." She experienced an uncharacteristic longing to bury her face in her hands and cry. "Mama, can you get him upstairs to change?"

Still in his pajamas, Marc was running the circle from the kitchen, through the dining room, into the living room and back to the kitchen, arms held out, pretending he was an airplane. Noelle glanced at the clock. She wore no makeup, had thrown her hair into a damp updo because tussling with Marc had robbed her of the time to dry it, and her blouse was stained with syrup.

Noelle went to answer the door and discovered not a driver, but Christian standing on her steps. His eyes narrowed when he caught sight of her, and she realized he'd never seen her in such disarray.

She gestured him in. "Good morning, Christian. Please come in. There's coffee in the kitchen." Behind her came Marc's protesting wail and her mother's warning tone. "As you can tell, my household is in chaos and I'm running late. I thought you were the driver I hired to take us to the airport. He was supposed to be here twenty minutes ago."

Rather than walk past her, Christian backed her against the entry wall and cupped her face in gentle hands. Her muscles went limp as his lips covered hers. The kiss was tender and full of longing. She opened to him, sliding her hands into his hair to keep their mouths fused together.

A low groan built in her chest. It was the first time he'd touched her like this since she'd broken off their engagement, and she felt like a spring flower coming to life after a long, harsh winter.

"Prince Papa." Marc's slippered feet thudded down the hall toward them.

Christian broke off the kiss and surveyed Noelle with enigmatic eyes before turning to scoop his son off the floor and lift him high above his head.

While her son shrieked in delight, Noelle put a hand to her chest and snatched several seconds to recover. In the long years apart from him, she'd forgotten that being kissed by Christian was an excellent way to begin her day.

As Christian set Marc back on his feet, Noelle nudged her son toward Mara. "Marc, please go upstairs with Nana and get dressed so we can be ready to leave if the car ever gets here."

"Noooo." And before Noelle could stop him, he'd bolted out the still-open front door, his howl fading as he raced away.

She started for the door, but Christian caught her arm. "I'll get him. Why don't you take a couple minutes and have some of that coffee you mentioned earlier."

"We're already running late. If we don't get going now, we'll miss the plane." She thought of the appointments set up for later that day and bit her lower lip in frustration.

"I'll get you there."

She shook her head. "I have a car coming."

"I mean to New York."

Behind him, Marc flashed by on the front lawn. Noelle was so focused on her annoyance with Marc that it took a moment for Christian's words to penetrate.

"How are you going to do that?"

His slow smile sent goose bumps racing over Noelle's skin. "I have a very luxurious private plane gassed up and waiting for us at the airport."

"Us?" What was he saying?

"I've cleared my schedule for the next few days so I could accompany you and Marc to New York. I thought that while you worked, Marc and I could play."

Instantly Noelle knew her son would love that. Spending time with his father had become something he now looked forward to, and it would ease Noelle's mind knowing Marc wouldn't be cooped up in a hotel room with a stranger their entire stay.

"I can't ask you to do that."

"You didn't. I volunteered."

Her mind flashed to the kiss a moment earlier. "I hope you understand I'm going on business. What just happened..." She made a vague gesture toward the spot where he'd pinned her to the wall and kissed her senseless. "I hope you don't think..."

The glow in his eyes told her that's exactly what he was thinking, but he shook his head. "I'm going to spend time with Marc. You don't need to worry that I'll distract you from any of your plans."

Oh, he'd distract her, all right. The craving to make love with him purred in her body like a contented cat. It would only be a matter of time before it woke and dug in its sharp claws.

"I guess then I can send the driver on his way."

"Already done."

Before she could protest his high-handedness, Christian was out the door.

"You'd better put on some makeup and fix your hair," Mara said, rich amusement in her voice. "Not that Prince Christian will care one way or another. He seems to approve of you no matter what."

Cheeks burning at her mother's teasing, Noelle raced upstairs to change out of her stained blouse and finish packing. If a couple new pieces of lingerie found their way into her suitcase as well as a sexy black lace nightgown, that didn't mean she had changed her mind about staying focused on business.

Since Christian was dressed casually in jeans and a gray sweater over a white collared shirt, Noelle decided against her original choice of a tailored burgundy suit and slipped into black skinny pants, a denim shirt and her favorite pair of black flats.

To show her mother that she didn't intend to go all out for Christian, Noelle applied black liner on her upper lids and enhanced her lips with a brilliant red. By the time she emerged from her bedroom with her suitcase, Christian had Marc dressed, his hair combed and teeth brushed. Noelle didn't marvel at how he'd accomplished so much in such a short period of time. She merely sent him a grateful look and headed downstairs.

Christian's driver fetched their suitcases while she settled Marc in the backseat and slid in after him. A moment later Christian joined them, his body solid and reassuring at her side. The worry and doubts that had plagued her these past few days abruptly lost their power. As the car began rolling down her driveway, Noelle sighed and squeezed Christian's arm.

"Thank you for coming with us."

He covered her hand and smiled. "No thanks necessary. I'm happy to be with you and Marc."

It wasn't a calculated line to impress her, but the unadorned truth. Noelle's heart expanded. Suddenly her decision to break off their engagement appeared like the worst one she'd ever made. Christian loved Marc. And she loved Christian. The truth flashed in her mind like a neon sign. Of course she loved him. She'd never stopped. For five years she'd ignored the truth by focusing on maintaining a balance between her career and being the best mom she could.

But her realization came too late. She'd already agreed to marry him and then called it off, freeing Christian from any moral obligation he might have felt toward her and Marc.

Christian tugged on the dark green scarf she'd knotted around her neck. "Where'd you go? You're a long way off."

"Sorry."

"Marc and I were just discussing our plans for New York. He's very excited to go to his first baseball game."

"I packed my glove," the boy announced. "So I can catch a home-run ball."

"Actually, we'll be sitting behind home plate so you'll have to catch a foul ball instead."

"Foul balls!" Marc exclaimed, kicking his feet. "And the zoo."

"Bronx or Central Park?" Christian asked.

"Both."

Noelle laughed. "You're going to be busy."

"It'll be fun. I've never had much opportunity to sight-see in New York. Every time I've been there it's been for business."

"I think I'm a little envious of you two," Noelle said and meant it. Ever since finding out she had an investor for her ready-to-wear line, she'd been caught up in all the deal's details. Now, she wished someone else could take care of business while she hung out with her two favorite men.

"Mama has to work." Marc grinned past her toward his father, and the two shared a special moment that excluded Noelle.

"Mama has to work," she agreed, so glad her son had this wonderful man in his life to love him.

# Eleven

When the pressure changed in the jet's cabin, Christian stretched his legs and glanced toward his son. Despite his excitement at visiting New York, Marc was a good traveler. Considering the boy's abundant energy, Christian had worried that Marc would be a restless terror. At the beginning of the flight, he'd settled right down with crayons and a coloring book. Later, Noelle and Christian had taken turns reading to him for an hour after which he'd had lunch, napped and was now quietly enjoying a Disney movie.

This had offered plenty of time for Noelle and Christian to talk. By mutual consent, they'd not strayed into any tricky personal topics while their son sat nearby. Instead, Noelle had laid out her business plan and asked Christian for feedback.

"Your third-year numbers seem a little conservative. Are you really convinced your business will grow at only seven percent?"

"Seven is a little above average and a safe estimate."

"You've never struck me as the sort who goes for safe." He hadn't imbued the comment with subtext, but Noelle's eyes narrowed.

"I have Marc to think about now. I can't jump into something if there seems to be some inherent risk involved." Although her tone was mild enough, tension formed little lines around her mouth.

"I understand." But Christian wasn't sure he did.

"Do you? Because doing what's best for him is my top priority."

Somehow they'd strayed from discussing business, and Christian had no idea what she was trying to tell him. "I understand." Repeating the words didn't have the effect he'd hoped.

Noelle grew even more agitated. "I know I've been hard on you. And I've been selfish."

Since it was obvious she had something to get off her chest, Christian kept his mouth shut and let her vent. She was beautiful, with her tantalizing lips painted bright red and the green of her scarf heightening the chestnut tones in her eyes. She'd kicked off her pointed black flats and sat with her feet tucked beneath her. The pen she'd been using to make notes was jabbed into her topknot for easy access. He wanted very badly to haul her onto his lap and kiss her silly.

"I want Marc to see you as a permanent fixture in his life."

All day she'd been swapping the engagement ring back and forth between her right and left hands. He doubted she was even aware that she was toying with the ring or that at the moment it rested on her left hand exactly where Christian wanted it.

"I thought that's what we've been doing with the dinners and outings."

"Yes." She kept her gaze trained on his shoulder. "But I think we should have something formal in place."

"A custody agreement?"

Her shoulders stiffened for a moment as if she were wincing from a blow. Christian could tell the offer wasn't easy for her. A second later she nodded.

"I think Marc will benefit from more time with his father."

"Not as much as his father will benefit." Christian kept his tone light to conceal his heavy heart. Always impatient, he wanted to claim both Noelle and Marc as his.

Noelle gave him a tremulous smile. "You always know just what to say."

"What sort of time did you have in mind for Marc to spend with me?"

"Obviously it will depend on your travel schedule. I thought maybe when we get back you could take him overnight and see how it goes."

"I didn't get a chance to tell you last week, but I've restructured some of my business dealings to keep me in Sherdana more. I'd like as much time with Marc as you're willing to give me." And with Noelle, but that didn't seem as likely now.

"That's wonderful. Seeing more of each other will only strengthen your relationship with Marc."

"And what are you planning to do with all your free time?"

Giving him partial custody would offer her a break from motherhood. An opportunity to date. Although he was convinced she wasn't in love with Geoff, he couldn't claim to know how the lawyer felt about Noelle. Suddenly Christian wasn't so sure he liked where things were heading.

She laughed. "I suspect for the next year or so, I'll be working around the clock to launch my ready-to-wear line and continue expanding my couture business. While he's with you, I won't have to worry that Marc is being neglected."

Christian considered what she'd said. It hadn't occurred to him that she'd feel guilty for working hard at her thriving business. "It will be good to have both of us there for him."

"You're right." She leaned forward, her expression earnest. "I didn't realize how much Marc needed a father until these past few weeks. I'm sorry I didn't tell you about him sooner."

Christian was touched by her apology but knew he couldn't let her take all the blame. "I never gave you any reason to think I would be there for Marc." He regretted missing Marc's first four years, but also for failing Noelle even as he thought he was trying to help her. "I wish I could take back the past five years."

Noelle shook her head. "I don't. If you hadn't broken things off I never would have gone to Paris and had a chance to learn under Matteo."

"And become an internationally famous wedding gown designer."

"You see. It all worked out perfectly in the end." But her smile wasn't as bright as her voice. "In the end you did me a huge favor."

Maybe he had, but Christian acknowledged that he'd also done himself a disservice by letting her go.

An exhausted Noelle returned to her suite at the Four Seasons after a grueling second day of meetings and interviews to find her son wearing a Yankees jersey and cap and carrying an autographed baseball in his mitt.

"And then he swung like this." Marc demonstrated a dramatic swing that spun him in a circle. "The ball went like…gone…gone…gone. Home run!" He threw his arms into the air and ran around the suite's living room as if running the bases.

"Goodness." Noelle looked to Christian, who stood with his hands in the back pockets of his jeans, watching his son with such fondness a lump formed in Noelle's throat. "Sounds like it was a fun game."

"It was grrreat." Marc charged toward Christian, who absorbed his son's enthusiastic hug with a grin. "And tomorrow we're going on a boat ride to the Statue of Liberty."

"You two are certainly taking advantage of all New York has to offer." Once again Noelle found herself regretting all the quality time she was missing with her son.

Christian picked up on the source of her melancholy as he swung Marc into his arms. "You could cancel your meetings and join us."

"Tempting." She smiled through her weariness. "But I only have tomorrow morning to get the last of the details hammered out."

"You're running yourself ragged."

"I know, but it will be worth it in the end." Satisfaction suffused her. As grinding as the pace had been since the jet's wheels had touched down on the New York runway, her ready-to-wear line was getting the right backing and garnering the perfect buzz.

"I'm really proud of you." While Noelle had been lost in thought, Christian had set down Marc and stepped close. "I want you to know that whatever you need I'll be here to help."

When his arm slid around her waist, drawing her against his body for a friendly hug, Noelle's pulse bucked. The man smelled like sunshine and soap. She longed to rest her cheek against the cotton stretched across his broad chest and let the world fade away. Her hunger for him flared. It had been a week since they'd made love, but with all that had happened in the meantime, it felt more like months.

Noelle leaned back and gazed up into Christian's molten gold eyes. Her knees weakened at the heat of his desire, and her lips parted as he lowered his head. A small body crashed against them, reminding Noelle that she and Christian weren't alone. She set her hand on Marc's head, frustration making the ache of longing that much more intense.

"What sort of plans do you have for dinner?" Christian asked, his arm sliding away from her body. He'd booked a suite at the Four Seasons in order to be close to his son. "Marc had a hot dog, popcorn and cotton candy at the ballpark, so I thought it would be a good idea to feed him a healthy dinner and we hoped you'd be able to join us."

As hard as it was to turn down the offer with two pairs of matching gold eyes trained on her, Noelle shook her head. "I'm having dinner with some designer friends of mine, and then there's a gala I'm attending afterward."

Marc showed less disappointment at this news than Christian. Their son was having far too much fun with his father to notice his mother's absence. As Marc dashed over to retrieve his mitt and autographed baseball from the coffee table, Christian's deep voice rumbled through her.

"I'm sorry you can't join us."

"So am I." And she meant it. "If it wasn't business…"

He nodded in understanding, his hands sliding into his pockets once more. "That's why you're here."

While part of Noelle appreciated his support, she couldn't stop wishing he'd ask her to cut her night short so she could tuck Marc into bed and maybe invite Christian to linger for some private time with her. Instead, he headed to his son, leaving her free to get ready for her evening out.

Three hours later, Noelle stood beside Victor, her mind far from business and the well-dressed crowd gathered to support a local food pantry. She was wondering if she could plead a headache and get back to the hotel in time to put her son to bed.

And the other thing…

All night long her heart and body had been wrestling with her mind regarding Christian. She longed to spend the night in his arms. To pretend she hadn't broken off their engagement in a foolish rush because she'd thought to beat him to the punch. But could she have married him thinking that he was merely following through on a contract he'd made with her? It had been one thing to marry him knowing he didn't love her when they were both taking steps to secure the future of the country.

"This has been a fantastic couple of days," Victor said, his enthusiasm dragging Noelle's attention back to the ballroom. "I think your line is going to be a huge success."

"Have I told you how much I appreciate all you've done?"

"I've just started things rolling."

"You've done more than that. You've created a tsunami of media interest and made sure that I'm meeting all the right people to make this line a success."

"I believe in you." Victor's shrewd brown eyes softened. "I wouldn't have partnered with you if I didn't. You're talented and business-savvy. It's been a pleasure working with you."

"It's been wonderful working with you, as well." Throat tight, she gave him a smile as she squeezed his hand. "Now, if you don't mind, I'm going to go back to the hotel and tuck my son into bed. I've neglected him terribly these past two days."

"I understand perfectly."

Noelle turned down Victor's offer of his car and left him to make her way out of the ballroom. It was nine-thirty, but she doubted Marc was in bed yet. She was in the process of sending Christian a text letting him know she was on her way back when someone behind her called her name. With a weary sigh, Noelle turned and spied a tall, bone-thin woman in her early thirties coming toward her, recognizing her as the *Charme* magazine editor who'd been overheard making disparaging remarks about her most recent fall couture collection. Not surprising, since she and Giselle had been rivals at Matteo Pizarro Designs and Giselle knew how to hold a grudge.

"Giselle, how lovely to see you." Noelle gave her former coworker a polite smile.

"I understand you and Prince Christian Alessandro are hot and heavy once more."

In the old days, before she'd realized what a snake Giselle could be, Noelle had told the seemingly sympathetic woman all about her two-year relationship with Christian. "We are friends." There was no way Noelle was going to tell the woman anything.

"Friendly enough that he accompanied you and your son to New York."

Although there had been speculation, the media hadn't yet discovered Christian's true relationship to Marc, and Noelle had no intention of sharing anything with Giselle.

"He's a friend," Noelle repeated, keeping her tone bland. "Now, if you'll excuse me, it's been a long couple of days." She turned to go, but Giselle's next words stopped her.

"I hear you're launching a ready-to-wear line."

Reminding herself that despite the animosity between

them, Giselle had an influential position in the industry, Noelle put on her interview face. "That's why I'm in New York. To meet with my backer and start making arrangements for manufacturing."

"Oh, Prince Christian isn't backing you?" Giselle's surprise didn't ring true. "I thought with you two being so close...and since he's helped you out before."

What was Giselle trying to get at?

"Prince Christian has never helped me."

When triumph flashed in Giselle's eyes, Noelle felt her uneasiness rise. Giselle had sabotaged her efforts several times when Noelle had first joined Matteo Pizarro Designs. Naively believing Giselle had been her friend had enabled the older woman to take credit for Noelle's ideas and ruin an entire week's worth of sketches before they were set to present their designs to Matteo as part of a special runway collection he was to exhibit at the Louvre. When, in the hour before they were to meet with Matteo, Noelle had crafted five sketches and Matteo had selected one of those, Giselle had been livid.

"You can tell the rest of the world such lies, but I know the truth."

"What truth?" Noelle knew better than to ask, but Giselle's absolute confidence had rattled her.

"That you never would have gotten the job with Matteo Pizarro without your prince's help."

"That's a lie."

"I heard Matteo speaking to Claudia about it. He said you were too inexperienced to hire, and he never would have considered you except that he was doing a favor for Prince Christian."

Noelle awakened to the truth as if she'd been slapped in the face. She'd been so shocked that she'd landed a position with such a prestigious designer. Her work was acceptable, but not outstanding. Only after she started working for Matteo Pizzaro and been inspired firsthand by the man's brilliance had she begun to gain confidence as a designer and take chances.

"It might be true," Noelle conceded, "but that's because Prince Christian believed in my talent before I did." And he'd see it as a great way to end their relationship.

But did that really make sense? Surely Christian had ended things with dozens of women without finding them a dream job that sent them five hundred miles away.

Giselle must have perceived Noelle's confusion as vulnerability because she stepped closer. "You'd be nothing if he hadn't used his influence to get Matteo to hire you."

"Maybe I wouldn't be a wedding gown designer to the wealthy and famous," Noelle agreed, no longer the naïve twenty-five-year-old girl Giselle had been able to take advantage of. "But I would still be the mother of an amazing little boy. And I'd be all the better for never having met you."

So much for playing nice with the media. Noelle turned on her heel and slipped from the ballroom, her heart racing after the ugly encounter. Her thoughts were a chaotic jumble as she slid into a cab for the two-mile trek back to the Four Seasons. She didn't doubt Giselle spoke the truth about Christian arranging for her to get the job with Matteo. What she couldn't sort out was how she felt about it.

Fifteen minutes later she let herself into her hotel suite, surprised to find Christian watching TV in her living room. There was no sign of Marc.

"You're back early," he said, using the remote to turn off the TV. He got to his feet as she crossed the room.

"I wanted to tuck Marc in, but it looks like I'm too late."

"He fell asleep on the couch around nine. The last two days have been pretty busy."

"You didn't have to stay. What happened to the nanny?"

"I sent her home. I have a couple things on my mind to talk to you about."

"I have something on my mind, as well."

Christian regarded her curiously as he gestured toward the sofa. When they were both seated, he said, "Do you want to begin?"

"I found out something tonight that I'd like you to confirm."

"Go ahead."

"Did you get me the job at Matteo Pizarro Designs?"

He looked startled, but whether by her question or the lack of accusation in her tone, Noelle couldn't guess.

"Yes."

"Why?"

"Because you were talented, and I knew you wanted it."

She shook her head. "And so you could break things off and not feel guilty?"

"I broke things off so you'd take the job."

Such altruism was not in keeping with his character, and Noelle wasn't sure she believed him. "You broke things off because you wanted to be with Talia."

He took Noelle's hand and lifted it to his right cheek. She touched the puckered skin of his scars. "How much do you remember about the night of my accident?"

Her first impulse was to pull away, but he held her fast. Christian wore his scars from that night on his skin. She wore hers inside. "We went to a party and I drank too much and got out of control because I thought you and Talia took off together."

"You didn't drink too much." Christian's expression hardened. "You were drugged."

"What?" The night had been unusually fuzzy, and she didn't remember more than one drink. But drugged? Why would he have kept something like this from her? "By whom?"

"Someone I thought was my friend." The anger in his voice was very real.

"Why?"

"You know how wild the crowd I ran with was. We treated the world like it was our playground, and we could do whatever we wanted without consequences. In contrast, you were sensible and worked hard at your career. The more involved I became with you, the less I saw them. They didn't like it very much, especially when I tried to bring you into our circle. They decided to go after you."

"By drugging me?" Noelle shivered as she realized just how vulnerable she'd been that night. She'd woken the next morning in her own bed with no idea how she'd gotten there. There'd been a video of her on the internet. She'd been dancing like a drunken fool. Because she couldn't remember any of it, she wasn't sure if she'd acted out because Christian had left with Talia or if he'd taken off because of how she'd been acting. "I thought you broke up with me because of how I behaved that night."

"I did. When I realized how much danger being with me had put you in." He shook his head. "They wanted you out of my life. It worked."

"But you left the party." She remembered being told that he was gone. Well, that wasn't quite true. Memories of the evening's events grew very indistinct after the first hour or so. The next morning the internet had lit up about the horrific car accident. There'd been no mention of a passenger, but she assumed the royal family simply covered that up.

"Because I thought you did. Talia used your phone to text me, saying that if I couldn't treat you any better then maybe one of your friends would. I chased after you and thought that you were leaving with Andre. At the time I didn't realize it was Talia. I followed them."

She couldn't grasp how his mind had been working that night. "You thought I left with Andre?" The skeptical laughter bubbling in her chest died beneath Christian's somber gaze. "How could you believe I would do that?"

"You'd been unhappy for a while. I thought perhaps you'd had enough."

"But to leave in the middle of a party after sending you a text? And with one of your friends?" It stung that he'd understood her so little. "You knew how I felt about you."

"Yes. But I let you think I wasn't exclusive even when I knew you weren't seeing anyone else."

His phrasing caught her attention. "You let me think? What does that mean? That you weren't seeing Talia and all the others you'd been photographed with?" Christian had never made excuses for his freewheeling lifestyle or said the sorts of things a girlfriend wanted to hear. Social media had buzzed with his exploits, and while that had hurt, Noelle had recognized that if she wanted him in her life, she had to share him.

"Not after the first few months. I didn't want to be with anyone but you." He rubbed his temples. "I hated that."

"Because I wasn't beautiful and exciting like all the other women you partied with?"

"You were both beautiful and exciting. But I didn't like having anyone relying on me for anything. And the way you looked at me…" He sighed. "Things were happening to me that I didn't like."

"Things?" she echoed, half afraid of what he might tell her. She'd mostly succeeded at never reading between the lines with Christian, knowing that way led to madness. But then he'd never been particularly vague. Voice light, she prompted, "What sort of things?"

A fissure formed in his granite expression. "Feelings."

"I can see why that upset you." She couldn't resist some faint mockery. It helped hide the pain his words caused.

Why had caring about her been something he'd been so unhappy about? At the time, she would have been thrilled beyond belief to think that she'd meant something more to him than just a tranquil pit stop in his eventful social life.

"I knew from the first that I wasn't good for you." He caressed her cheek with his knuckles. "Instead of taking your talent to Paris or London, you stayed in your tiny Carone flat, working for a man who claimed your designs as his own. Being with me kept you stuck. That's why I encouraged you to send off your résumé and portfolio."

"It wasn't your fault that I was afraid." Of taking a chance with her career and finding out she couldn't compete. Of losing the man she loved. "I just wasn't ready to leave Sherdana."

"But once you thought we'd broken up, you jumped at the chance to interview for a position at Matteo Pizarro."

"That's not fair. When I thought you'd chosen Talia, I knew I had to get away from Sherdana." It wasn't until she'd settled in Paris months later and discovered Christian and Talia weren't together that Noelle recognized her insecurities had worked against her.

"Exactly my point. Even after you got the job with Matteo Pizarro, you hesitated."

She'd paused in the middle of packing and visited him in the hospital, hoping he would ask her to stay. He'd been so cold. "You told me you'd moved on."

"Would you have left if I hadn't?"

She couldn't meet his eyes. "I wanted to be with you."

"And being with me caused you to be in danger. For your own good I sent you away."

"What would you have done if I'd told you I was pregnant?"

Christian shook his head. "I'd like to believe I would've done the right thing, but I honestly don't know."

"What would have been the right thing?"

"Marry you. Settle down. Become a good husband and father."

Noelle couldn't stop the wry smile that curved her lips. "Neither one of us was ready for that."

The way his eyebrows shot up said she'd surprised him. "You were."

"I was happy in Paris. I loved what I was doing. It was hard to manage my career and being a new mom, but I discovered such satisfaction in my ability to do both."

"See, breaking up with me was the best thing that could have happened to you."

"That's not true." But she couldn't deny that in many ways he'd done her a favor.

"So what happens now?"

"Now?"

"I'm no longer a young, irresponsible cad. You are thriving in your career and as a mother. We've demonstrated that the chemistry between us is hotter than ever. I have a son that I love, and want to be a full-time father. Marry me."

She saw what he was offering and spun the large diamond ring on her finger. He'd always been what she wanted. So, why couldn't she just say yes?

# Twelve

Christian saw Noelle's hesitation and felt his heart tear.

"Victor convinced me to move to New York for the next six months so I can focus on the ready-to-wear line."

"Victor convinced you?" Christian probed her expression. "Or did you have this in mind before you left Sherdana?"

"A little of both," she admitted. "Thanks to you Marc loves it here, and I don't know how I'm supposed to take care of all the manufacturing issues and marketing details if I'm in Europe."

"You let me believe that I would have partial custody of Marc. Have you changed your mind?"

"No. We will figure something out about that."

"But you and I won't be together."

She stared at her hands and shook her head. "Being Marc's parents and having great sexual chemistry aren't strong enough reasons to get married. I don't want to get divorced in a few years because the only time we're compatible is in bed."

"I don't plan to divorce." Just the thought made his chest ache. "I intend to spend the rest of my life with you."

Again she didn't answer right away. If her goal was to convince him that she didn't share his commitment, he refused to let her succeed. Pushed to fight for the woman he wanted, Christian stood and scooped Noelle into his arms. He silenced her protests with a fierce glare and marched toward her bedroom. Setting her on her feet near the bed, he shut the door and stripped off his shirt before turning to face her.

"Christian, this isn't going to change my mind about staying in New York." So she said, but her gaze roamed his bare torso in hungry desperation.

"I have no intention of talking you out of moving to New York." He eliminated the distance between them with deliberate strides, letting passion incinerate his fear of losing her. "I only want what's best for you."

He hadn't meant for his words to upset her, but suddenly she looked stricken. Moving with slow tenderness, he slipped the dress from her body and worshipped her soft skin with his fingers and lips. The catch on her strapless bra popped free, no match for his expertise, and she sucked in a sharp breath as he took one breast in his hand.

With his desire spiraling in ever tightening circles, Christian dropped to his knees before Noelle and hooked his fingers in her white, lacy panties, pulling them down her thighs. The vibration in her muscles increased, threatening her stability. To keep her upright, he framed her slender hips with his hands. Her flat stomach quivered as he trailed kisses across it.

He'd missed the chance to watch her belly grow round with his son. He set his forehead against her, overwhelmed by how much more he stood to lose if he couldn't win her love. His sudden stillness prompted her to ride her palms across his bare shoulders and dragged her nails through his hair. He wrapped his arms around her and set his cheek against her abdomen.

"Christian?"

He'd never fully appreciated the power of her soothing touch. How her quiet voice and fervent embrace created a sanctuary that let his worries slip away.

"I wasn't completely truthful when I said I only wanted what was best for you. What I really want is what's best for me. And that's you."

"Make love to me."

Not needing to be asked twice, Christian lifted her off her feet and set her on the mattress. Together they stripped the comforter away, exposing the cool sheets. Noelle knelt on the bed and snagged the waistband of his trousers, drawing him toward her. Moving with confidence, she unfastened his belt and slid down his zipper until she'd freed him.

He had the package open and the condom ready, but when she began to slide it down his erection, the heaven of her strong fingers closed around him ripped a groan from his lips. Rolling her fingers over his sensitive tip, she gave a half smile as his hips bucked forward. Shuddering, too aroused to withstand her ministrations for long, Christian sucked in a sharp breath and freed himself from her grasp.

"You drive me crazy," he growled a second before claiming her lips in a hot, fiery kiss.

Tenderness vanished beneath the onslaught of her answering passion as she pushed her breasts against his chest and drove him crazy with the seductive sway of her hips. Filling his hands with her adorable butt, he shifted her off the mattress and coaxed her thighs around his waist. With his erection hardened to the point of pain, he laid her on the crisp sheets and moved between her thighs.

But he didn't enter her as she'd expected. Instead, his lips grazed over her mound, causing her head to lift off the bed and her gaze to sharpen. Enjoying the play of emotion on her face, he dipped his tongue into her sizzling heat and tasted her arousal. With a groan, her head fell back and her hips strained forward. Christian grinned as he began again, finding the rhythm that she liked and coaxing her toward climax.

She came against his mouth, her back arching, his name on her lips. In the aftermath, she lay with her eyes closed, her chest rising and falling with each unsteady breath. Smiling, Christian kissed his way back up her body. He settled between her thighs and kissed her with all the longing that filled his heart. Then, at her urging, he eased into her tight heat. She burrowed her fingers in his hair and set the soles of her feet on the mattress, tipping her hips to meet his slow, deep thrust.

Now it was his turn to cry out. Burying his face in her neck, he began to move. Pleasure swept over him in a stormy rush. He set his teeth against the glorious friction, fighting against the orgasm that threatened to claim him. By slowing his movements, he was able to regain some control, but the provocative sweep of Noelle's hands over his hot skin wasn't making things any easier.

"Faster," she murmured, her teeth catching at his earlobe. "I want you to come hard." Her throaty voice and the flick of her tongue over the tender spot where she'd nipped him caused him to shudder and almost lose control.

"Damn it, stop that," he growled, cupping one butt cheek and adjusting his angle just a bit to allow his pelvis to rub her just so.

With her eyes closed and her lips curled into a satisfied grin, she yielded to his pace. Content to watch her, Christian barely noticed the heat building in his groin until it threatened to engulf him.

"Come with me," Christian said. It was a plea rather than a command.

He thrust more powerfully. Her lashes lifted and her eyes met his. This is what they were good at. Connecting at this intimate level. Her vulnerability had taught him openness. Her strength had made it safe for him to let go. She'd never judged or demanded. Just given. It had made him want to give in return.

Fighting against his orgasm until she started to go over the edge, Christian felt something inside him struggling to get free. Noelle's beautiful eyes widened as the first spasms of her climax began. Wild with relief, Christian drove forward into his own release, the force of it ripping a harsh cry from him. Blackness snatched at him as stars exploded behind his eyes. Dimly he heard Noelle call his name.

For what felt like an eternity, wave after wave of pleasure pounded him. At last there was only peace and ragged breathing. Weak and shaky, Christian shifted his weight off Noelle and gathered her into his arms. She returned his hearty embrace with matching energy. They lay entwined for several minutes before Christian went to the bathroom and came back with a towel and her nightgown.

She'd never liked sleeping naked, which was fine with him because he enjoyed gliding his hands over her silk covered curves and stripping her bare each time they made love. Once her glorious breasts, tiny waist and slender hips were concealed beneath the pale green fabric, Christian set the alarm on his phone to wake them at 5:00 a.m. and pulled the covers up over them both.

This would be the first time they spent the night together since reconnecting, and Noelle's lack of protest made Christian wonder if she'd changed her mind about his proposal. If he could spend the rest of his life with Noelle, he would be happier than he deserved to be.

He stopped resisting the pull of exhaustion. Keeping up with Marc's boundless energy had taken its toll. Content in a way he hadn't been for a long time, Christian buried his nose in Noelle's fragrant hair and sighed.

"I love you," he murmured and drifted off to sleep.

Christian's words lanced through Noelle, shocking her to complete wakefulness. Before the echo of his voice faded, his deep breathing told her he was unconscious. Her first impulse was to shake him awake and force him to repeat the words. Had he meant them? Had he even realized what he said? Why was it the man couldn't speak his heart unless he was semiconscious?

Noelle lay awake for a long time, her cheek on Christian's bare chest, listening to the steady thump of his heart. She pondered the impact her expanding business was about to have on her son and her love life. Was it wrong to want it all? Success with her ready-to-wear line? The family she'd longed for with Christian? The thought of reaching out and grabbing nothing but air worried her, but she wouldn't see stars without overcoming a fear of the dark.

No solutions revealed themselves that night. She awoke to an empty bed and a brief note on hotel stationery from Christian, letting her know he had taken Marc to his suite so she could get ready in peace. The note was brisk and informative, lacking the romantic overtones left over from the previous night.

Heaving a sigh, Noelle got up and went to shower. Had all her what-ifs and how-tos from the previous night been a waste of time? Perhaps in the hazy aftermath of some spectacular lovemaking she'd only imagined what she longed to hear Christian say.

No. Noelle refused to believe that. She knew what she'd heard. Christian loved her. Based on how he'd protected her from his friends and pulled strings to get her on the path to a fabulous career, he'd loved her for a long time. That he had a hard time being vulnerable didn't surprise her.

Not only had he run with a condescending group of entitled troublemakers who tormented anyone who showed weakness, he'd also been the youngest of three princes, far from the throne with no expectations placed on him. Christian had once shared that he often felt like an afterthought. Noelle suspected this was what had led him to act out.

On the way to her first meeting, Noelle called her assistant back in Sherdana to check on her appointment for later in the week and was delighted to learn that the bride had postponed until the following month. This opened up the rest of the week, and more than anything Noelle wanted a quiet dinner with Christian and to spend a day roaming New York City with him and their son.

Knowing that Christian had cleared his entire schedule so he could be there for Marc, she sent him a text asking if they could postpone returning to Sherdana. He responded with a photo of him and Marc cheek to cheek, both giving a thumbs-up. Warmth spread through her, and she clutched the screen to her chest. Loosing a ragged sigh, she sent back a smiley face and spent the rest of the ride organizing a romantic dinner for two.

At a little after four in the afternoon, Christian carried his sleeping son across the Four Seasons lobby and into an elevator. Along the way he caught several women watching him, their expressions reading *isn't that sweet*. He resisted smiling until the elevator doors closed. He wasn't accustomed to women approving of his deeds and found he rather liked it.

Noelle was working at the desk in her suite when he let himself in. She started to rise, but he waved her back. In the past couple of days, he'd grown accustomed to caring for Marc and enjoyed it a great deal.

After taking his son's shoes off and tucking him beneath a light blanket with his favorite stuffed dinosaur, Christian returned to the living room. Noelle had put away her laptop and was standing near the wide windows staring out over the city. As Christian drew near, she smiled at him over her shoulder.

"Another hectic day?"

"I don't think there's a single question about the Statue of Liberty that Marc didn't ask."

"I'm sure." She leaned her head back against Christian's shoulder as he slipped his arms around her. He felt more than heard her sigh. "I love you."

Unsure if he'd heard her correctly, Christian held perfectly still, afraid to say anything and ruin the moment.

"But I think you already know that," she continued.

"I don't. I didn't." Chest aching, he turned her to face him. "I love you, too. You know that, right?"

She smiled at his earnest tone. "I didn't until you told me just before you fell asleep last night."

"I'm sorry it took me so long to say it. Those three words have played through my mind a hundred times over the past week. A thousand times since we first met. I guess I've avoided the truth for so long that it became a habit to hide it from you, as well."

"You're not the only one who has trouble breaking old patterns of behavior. I ended our engagement because I didn't believe you could possibly want me as something other than the mother of your son."

Cupping her face in his hands, heart racing to the point where he was light-headed, Christian searched her expression. "Does that mean you've changed your mind about wanting to marry me?" He sounded neither calm nor casual as he asked the question. To his relief she didn't leave him in suspense for long.

"I've always wanted to marry you," she teased. "Nothing could change that."

No longer capable of holding back his impatience, Christian put his hands on her shoulders and gave her a little shake. "Are you going to marry me?"

"Yes!" She threw her arms around his waist and lifted her lips to receive his kiss.

Christian wasted no time letting her know how delighted he was by her decision. One ravenous, joyful kiss followed another until a weight struck their legs. Setting Noelle's lips free, Christian glanced down at his son. Noelle's hand was already smoothing the sleep-tossed waves of Marc's dark brown hair.

"Mama, I'm hungry."

Snatching breath back into his lungs, Christian chuckled. "How is that possible after everything he's eaten today?"

"He has a lot of growing to do before he'll be as big as his father, and that takes fuel."

Christian bent and hoisted his son into his arms. Marc wrapped one arm around each of his parents as they stood close together.

"Your mother and I are getting married so the three of us can be a family," he said, catching a glimpse of Noelle's nod. "What do you think about that?" It was risky to ask a four-year-old such an important question when his stomach was empty, but Christian refused to wait another minute before making the engagement official. And telling Marc was as official as it got.

"Yeah. Will I get to live at the palace?" A couple weeks earlier it was the last place he'd wanted to visit, but now that he'd met his cousins and explored some of the rooms, he'd become much more interested in making it his home.

"Sometimes we can spend time there…" Noelle began, shooting Christian a quick frown.

Marc squirmed in Christian's grasp, his hunger once again snagging his attention. "May I have some cheese?"

Noelle made Marc a snack out of supplies stocked in the small refrigerator. When her son was content, she turned to Christian once more.

"Where are we going to live? The farmhouse is too small. Your apartment in Old Town has no outside space for Marc to play."

"I am in negotiations for an estate about twelve miles from the center of Carone. When I first learned about Marc, I decided he'd need more space than I currently have. If you approve of it, we can live there." He paused, wondering if she'd forgotten last night's decision to live in New York for six months. "As for the time you're planning to spend here, we can always rent an apartment near Central Park."

"We?" She looked hopeful.

"Before my brothers chose love over duty to the Sherdanian throne, I'd been considering expanding my ventures into the US. This seems like an excellent time to explore new territory."

Almost before he finished speaking, Noelle wrapped her arms tightly around his waist and pressed her cheek to his chest. "I'm so relieved to hear you say that. I didn't know how I was going to live apart from you these next six months."

Christian hugged her in return. "You didn't seriously think I was going to let you get away a second time, did you?"

She tipped back her head and gave him a wry smile. "Get away?"

"You have no idea what it cost me to let you go."

The torment in his voice made her shiver. She pulled him down for a kiss. Mindful of Marc's presence, they kept it affectionate and light. There would be plenty of time for passion later when they were alone.

As soon as Marc finished his snack, Christian lifted him into his arms and pulled out his cell phone. Earlier that day he'd realized that as many pictures as he'd taken with his son these past few days, not one of them had included Noelle. As the three of them clustered together in front of the window overlooking the New York skyline, Christian snapped their photo and sent it to his parents and brothers with the message that he and Noelle were engaged. Despite the time difference, he received immediate congratulations from everyone.

"It's official," he warned her. "There's no backing out now."

She regarded him with sparkling eyes. "You almost sound worried that I might."

"I learned the hard way never to take you for granted." He kissed her temple. "That will not happen again."

"We've both made mistakes and learned from them. I can see us making more."

"But as long as we don't let doubts come between us, we'll be just fine."

"Better than fine," she said, resting her head against his

shoulder and watching Marc put together a puzzle of the Statue of Liberty. "We're going to be gloriously happy."

Christian's arm tightened around Noelle. "That, my dazzling wife-to-be, sounds just about perfect."

\* \* \* \* \*

*Don't miss the first two novels*
*in the SHERDANA ROYALS series from*
*Cat Schield!*

*ROYAL HEIRS REQUIRED*
*A ROYAL BABY SURPRISE*

*And pick up these other emotional and sexy reads from*
*Cat Schield:*

*AT ODDS WITH THE HEIRESS*
*A MERGER BY MARRIAGE*
*A TASTE OF TEMPTATION*

*All available now, only from Harlequin Desire!*

\* \* \*

*Read on for an exclusive sneak preview of*
*ONE NIGHT CHARMER*
*from USA TODAY bestselling author Maisey Yates and*
*HQN Books!*

\* \* \*

*If you're on Twitter, tell us what you think of*
*Harlequin Desire! #harlequindesire*

*Copper Ridge, Oregon's, favorite bachelor is
about to meet his match!*

*If the devil wore flannel, he'd look like Ace Thompson.
He's gruff. Opinionated. Infernally hot. The last person
Sierra West wants to ask for a bartending job—not that
she has a choice. Ever since discovering that her
"perfect" family is built on a lie, Sierra has been
determined to make it on her own. Resisting her new
boss should be easy when they're always bickering.
Until one night, the squabbling stops...and something
far more dangerous takes over.*

*Ace has a personal policy against messing around with
staff—or with spoiled rich girls. But there's a steel
backbone beneath Sierra's silver-spoon upbringing.
She's tougher than he thought, and so much more
tempting. Enough to make him want to break all
his rules, even if it means risking his heart...*

*Read on for this special extended excerpt from
ONE NIGHT CHARMER
by USA TODAY bestselling author Maisey Yates.*

# CHAPTER ONE

THERE WERE TWO people in Copper Ridge, Oregon, who—between them—knew nearly every secret of every person in town. The first was Pastor John Thompson, who heard confessions of sin and listened to people pour out their hearts when they were going through trials and tribulations.

The second was Ace Thompson, owner of the most popular bar in town, son of the pastor and probably the least likely to attend church on Sunday or any other day.

There was no question that his father knew a lot of secrets, though Ace was pretty certain he himself got the more honest version. His father spent time standing behind the pulpit; Ace stood behind a bar. And there he learned the deepest and darkest situations happening in the lives of other townspeople while never revealing any of his own. He supposed, pastor or bartender, that was kind of the perk.

They poured it all out for you, and you got to keep your secrets bottled up inside.

That was how Ace liked it. Every night of the week, he had the best seat in the house for whatever show Copper Ridge wanted to put on. And he didn't even have to pay for it.

And with his newest acquisition, the show was about to get a whole lot better.

"Really?" Jack Monaghan sat down at the bar, beer in

hand, his arm around his new fiancée, Kate Garrett. "A mechanical bull?"

"That's right, Monaghan. This is a classy establishment, after all."

"Seriously," Connor Garrett said, taking the seat next to Jack, followed by his wife, Liss. "Where did you get that thing?"

"I traded it. Guy down in Tolowa owed me some money and he didn't have it. So he said I could come by and look at his stash of trash. Lo and behold, I discovered Ferdinand over there."

"Congratulations," Kate said. "I didn't think anything could make this place more of a dive. I was wrong."

"You're a peach, Kate," Ace said.

The woman smiled broadly and wrapped her arm around Jack's, leaning in and resting her cheek on his shoulder.

"Can we get a round?" Connor asked.

Ace continued to listen to their conversation as he served up their usual brew, enjoying the happy tenor of the conversation, since the downers would probably be around later to dish out woe while he served up harder liquor. The Garretts were good people, he mused. Always had been. Both before he'd left Copper Ridge, and since he'd come back.

His focus was momentarily pulled away when the pretty blonde who'd been hanging out in the dining room all evening drinking with friends approached the aforementioned Ferdinand.

He hadn't had too many people ride the bull yet, and he had to admit, he was finding it a pretty damn enjoyable novelty.

The woman tossed her head, her tan cowboy hat staying in place while her blond curls went wild around her shoulders. She wrapped her hands around the harness on top of the mechanical creature and hoisted herself up. Her movements were unsteady, and he had a feeling, based on the amount of time the group had been here, and how often the men in the group had come and gone from the bar, that she was more than a little bit tipsy.

Best seat in the house. He always had the best seat in the house.

She glanced up as she situated herself and he got a good look at her face. There was a determined glint in her eyes, her brows locked together, her lips pursed into a tight circle. She wasn't just tipsy, she was pissed. Looking down at the bull like it was her own personal Everest and she was determined to conquer it along with her rage. He wondered what a bedazzled little thing like her had to be angry about. A broken nail, maybe. A pair of shoes that she really wanted that was unavailable in her size.

She nodded once, her expression growing even *more* determined as she signaled the employee Ace had operating the controls tonight.

Ace moved nearer to the bar, planting his hands flat on the surface. "This probably won't end well."

The patrons at the bar turned their heads toward the scene. And he noticed Jack's posture go rigid. "Is that—"

"Yes," Kate said.

The mechanical bull pitched forward and the petite blonde sitting on top of it pitched right along with it. She managed to stay seated, but in Ace's opinion that was a miracle. The bull went back again, and the woman straightened, arching her back and thrusting her breasts forward, her head tilted upward, the overhead lighting bathing her pretty face in a golden glow. And for a moment, just a moment, she looked like a graceful, dirty angel getting into the rhythm of the kind of riding Ace preferred above anything else.

Then the great automated beast pitched forward again and the little lady went over the top, down onto the mats underneath. There were howls from her so-called friends as they enjoyed her deposition just a little too much.

She stood on shaky legs and walked back over to the group, picking up a shot glass and tossing back another, her face twisted into an expression that suggested this was not typical behavior for her.

Kate frowned and got up from her stool, making her way over to the other woman.

Ace had a feeling he should know the woman's name, had a feeling that he probably did somewhere in the back corner of his mind. He knew everyone. Which meant that he knew a lot *about* a lot of people, recognized nearly every face he passed on the street. He could usually place them with their most defining life moments, as those were the things that often spilled out on the bar top after a few shots too many.

But it didn't mean he could put a name to every face. There were simply too many of them.

"Who is that?" he asked.

"Sierra West," Jack said, something strange in his tone.

"Oh, right."

He knew the West family well enough, or rather, he knew of them. Everyone did. Though they were hardly the type to frequent his establishment. Sierra did, which would explain why she was familiar, though they never made much in the way of conversation. She was the type who was always absorbed in her friends or her cell phone when she came to place her order. No deep confessionals from Sierra over drinks.

He'd always found it a little strange she patronized his bar when the rest of the West family didn't.

Dive bars weren't really their thing.

He imagined mechanical bulls probably weren't, either. Judging not just on Sierra's pedigree, but on the poor performance.

"No cotillions going on tonight, I guess," Ace said.

Jack turned his head sharply, his expression dark. "What's that supposed to mean?"

"Nothing."

He didn't know why, but his statement had clearly offended Monaghan. Ace wasn't in the business of voicing his opinion. He was in the business of listening. Listening and serving. No one needed to know his take on a damn thing. They just wanted a sounding board to voice their own opinions and hear them echoed back.

Typically, he had no trouble with that. This had been a little slipup.

"She's not so bad," Jack said.

Sierra was a friend of Jack's fiancée, that much was obvious. Kate was over there talking to her, expression concerned. Sierra still looked mutinous. Ace was starting to wonder if she was mad at the entire world, or if something in particular had set her off.

"I'm sure she isn't." He wasn't sure of any such thing. In fact, if he knew one thing about the world and all the people in it, it was that there was a particular type who used their every advantage in life to take whatever they wanted, whenever they wanted it, regardless of promises made. Whether they were words whispered in the dark or vows spoken in front of whole crowds of loved ones.

He was a betting man. And he would lay odds that Sierra West was one of those people. She was the type. Rich, a big fish in the small pond of the community and beauti-

ful. That combination pretty much guaranteed her whatever she wanted. And when the option for *whatever you
wanted* was available, very few people resisted it.

Hell, why would you? There were a host of things he
would change if he had infinite money and power.

But just because he figured he'd be in the same boat
if he were rich and almighty didn't mean he had to like
it on others.

HE LOOKED BACK over at Kate, who patted her friend on
the shoulder before shaking her head and walking back
toward the group. "She didn't want to come sit with us or
anything," Kate said, looking frustrated.

The Garrett-Monaghan crew lingered at the bar for another couple of hours before they were replaced by another set of customers. Sierra's group thinned out a little
bit, but didn't disperse completely. A couple of the guys
were starting to get rowdy, and Ace was starting to think
he was going to have to play the part of his own bouncer
tonight. It wouldn't be the first time.

Fortunately, the noisier members of the group slowly
trickled outside. He watched as Sierra got up and made
her way back to the bathroom, leaving a couple of girls—
one of whom he assumed was the designated driver—sitting at the table.

The tab was caught up, so he didn't really care how it
all went down. He wasn't a babysitter, after all.

He turned, grabbed a rag out of the bucket beneath the
counter and started to wipe it down. When he looked up
again, the girls who had been sitting at the table were gone,
and Sierra West was standing in the center of the room
looking around like she was lost.

Then she glanced his way, and her eyes lit up like a sin-
ner looking at salvation.

*Wrong guess, honey.*

She wandered over to the bar, her feet unsteady. "Did you see where my friends went?"

She had that look about her. Like a lost baby deer. All wide, dewy eyes and unsteady limbs. And damned if she wasn't cute as hell.

"Out the door," he said, almost feeling sorry for her. Almost.

She wasn't the first pretty young drunk to get ditched in his bar by stupid friends. She was also exactly the kind of woman he avoided at all costs, no matter how cute or seemingly vulnerable she was.

"What?" She swayed slightly. "They weren't supposed to leave me."

She sounded mystified. Completely dumbfounded that anyone would ever leave her high and dry.

"I figured," he said. "Here's a tip—get better friends."

She frowned. "They're the best friends I have."

He snorted. "That's a sad story."

She held up her hand, the broad gesture out of place coming from such a refined creature. "Just a second."

"Sure."

She turned away, heading toward the door and out to the parking lot.

He swore. He didn't know if she had a car out there, but she was way too skunked to drive.

"Watch the place, Jenna," he said to one of the waitresses, who nodded and assumed a rather important-looking position with her hands flat on the bar and a rag in her hand, as though she were ready to wipe crumbs away with serious authority.

He rounded the counter and followed the same path Sierra had just taken out into the parking lot. He looked around for a moment and didn't see her. Then he looked down and there she was, sitting on the edge of the curb. "Everything okay?"

That was a stupid question; he already knew the answer.

She looked up. "No."

He let out a long-drawn-out sigh. The problem was, he'd followed her out here. If he had just let her walk out the door, then nothing but the pine trees and the seagulls would have been responsible for her. But no, he'd had to follow. He'd been concerned about her driving. And now he would have to follow through on that concern.

"You don't have a ride?"

She shook her head, looking miserable. "Everyone left me. Because they aren't nice. You're right. I do need better friends."

"Yes," he said, "you do. And let me go ahead and tell you right now, I won't be one of them. But as long as you don't live somewhere ridiculous like Portland, I can give you a ride home."

And this, right here, was the curse of owning a bar. Whether he should or not, he felt responsible in these situations. She was compromised, it was late, and she was alone. He could not let her meander her way back home. Not when he could easily see that she got there safely.

"A ride?" She frowned, her delicate features lit dramatically by the security light hanging on the front of the bar.

"I know your daddy probably told you not to take rides from strangers, but trust me, I'm the safest bet around. Unless you want to call someone." He checked his watch. "It's inching close to last call. I'm betting not very many people are going to come out right now."

She shook her head slowly. "Probably not."

He sighed heavily, reaching into his pocket and wrapping his fingers around his keys. "All right, come on. Get in the truck."

Sierra looked up at her unlikely, bearded, plaid-clad savior. She knew who he was, of course. Ace Thompson was the owner of the bar, and she bought beer from him at least twice a month when she came out with her friends. They'd exchanged money and drinks across the counter more times than she could recall, but this was more words than she'd ever exchanged with him in her life.

She was angry at herself. For getting drunk. For going out with the biggest jerks in the local rodeo club. For getting on the back of a mechanical bull and opening herself up to their derision—because honestly, when you put your drunk self up on a fake, bucking animal, you pretty much deserved it. And most of all, for sitting down in the parking lot acting like she was going to cry just because she had been ditched by said jerky friends.

Oh, and being *caught* at what was most definitely an epic low made it all even worse. He'd almost certainly seen her inglorious dismount off the mechanical bull, then witnessed everyone leaving without her.

She'd been so sure today couldn't get any worse.

She'd been wrong.

"I'm fine," she said, and she could have bitten off her own tongue, because she wasn't fine. As much as she wanted to pretend she didn't need his help, she kind of did. Granted, she could call Colton or Madison. But if her sister had to drive all the way down to town from the family estate she would probably kill Sierra. And if she called Colton's house his fiancée would probably kill Sierra.

Either way, that made for a dead Sierra.

She wasn't speaking to her father. Which, really, was the root of today's evil.

"Sure you are. *Most* girls who end up sitting on their behinds at 1:00 a.m. in a parking lot are just fine."

She blinked, trying to bring his face into focus. He refused to be anything but a fuzzy blur. "I am."

For some reason, her stubbornness was on full display, and most definitely outweighed her common sense. That was probably related to the alcohol. And to the fact that all of her restraint had been torn down hours ago. Sometime early this morning when she had screamed at her father and told him she never wanted to see him again, because she'd found out he was a liar. A cheater.

Right, so that was probably why she was feeling rebellious. Angry in general. But she probably shouldn't direct it at the person who was offering a helping hand.

"Don't make me ask you twice, Sierra. It's going to make me get real grumpy, and I don't think you'll like that." Ace shifted his stance, crossing his arms over his broad chest—she was pretty sure it was broad, either that or she was seeing double—and looked down at her.

She got to her wobbly feet, pitching slightly to the side before steadying herself. Her head was spinning, her stomach churning, and she was just mad. Because she felt like crap. Because she knew better than to drink like this, at least when she wasn't in the privacy of her own home.

"Which truck?" she asked, rubbing her forehead.

He turned, not waiting for her, and began to walk across the parking lot. She followed as quickly as she could. Fortunately, the lot was mostly empty, so she didn't have to watch much but the back of Ace as they made their way to the vehicle. It wasn't a new, flashy truck. It was old, but it was in good condition. Better than most she'd seen at such an advanced age. But then, Ace wasn't a rancher. He owned a bar, so it wasn't like his truck saw all that much action.

She stood in front of the passenger-side door for a long moment before realizing he was not coming around to open it for her. Her face heated as she jerked open the door for herself and climbed up inside.

It had a bench seat. And she found herself clinging to the door, doing her best to keep the expansive seat between them as wide as possible. She was suddenly conscious of the fact that he was a very large man. Tall, broad, muscular. She'd known that, somewhere in the back of her mind. But the way he filled up the cab of a truck containing just the two of them was much more significant than the way he filled the space in a vast and crowded bar.

He started the engine, saying nothing as he put the truck in Reverse and began to pull out of the lot. She looked straight ahead, desperate to find something to say. The silence was oppressive, heavy around them. It made her feel twitchy, nervous. She always knew what to say. She was in command of every social situation she stepped into. People found her charming, and if they didn't, they never said otherwise. Because she was Sierra West, and her family name carried with it the burden of mandatory respect from the people of Copper Ridge.

She took a deep breath, trying to ease the pressure in her chest, trying to remove the weight that was sitting there.

"What's your sign?" Somehow, her fuzzy brain had retrieved that as a conversation starter. The moment the words left her mouth she wanted to stuff them back in and swallow them.

To her surprise, he laughed. "Caution."

"What?"

"I'm a caution sign, baby. And it would be in your best interest to obey the warning…"

*Don't miss what happens when Sierra doesn't heed his advice in*
*ONE NIGHT CHARMER*
*by USA TODAY bestselling author Maisey Yates!*

# COMING NEXT MONTH FROM

## HARLEQUIN® Desire

### Available May 10, 2016

# REQUEST YOUR FREE BOOKS!
## 2 FREE NOVELS PLUS 2 FREE GIFTS!

**H** HARLEQUIN®

*Desire*

### ALWAYS POWERFUL, PASSIONATE AND PROVOCATIVE

**YES!** Please send me 2 FREE Harlequin® Desire novels and my 2 FREE gifts (gifts are worth about $10). After receiving them, if I don't wish to receive any more books, I can return the shipping statement marked "cancel." If I don't cancel, I will receive 6 brand-new novels every month and be billed just $4.55 per book in the U.S. or $5.24 per book in Canada. That's a savings of at least 13% off the cover price! It's quite a bargain! Shipping and handling is just 50¢ per book in the U.S. and 75¢ per book in Canada.* I understand that accepting the 2 free books and gifts places me under no obligation to buy anything. I can always return a shipment and cancel at any time. Even if I never buy another book, the two free books and gifts are mine to keep forever.

225/326 HDN GH2P

Name _____ (PLEASE PRINT) _____

Address _____ Apt. # _____

City _____ State/Prov. _____ Zip/Postal Code _____

Signature (if under 18, a parent or guardian must sign)

### Mail to the **Reader Service:**
**IN U.S.A.:** P.O. Box 1867, Buffalo, NY 14240-1867
**IN CANADA:** P.O. Box 609, Fort Erie, Ontario L2A 5X3

**Want to try two free books from another line?**
**Call 1-800-873-8635 or visit www.ReaderService.com.**

\* Terms and prices subject to change without notice. Prices do not include applicable taxes. Sales tax applicable in N.Y. Canadian residents will be charged applicable taxes. Offer not valid in Quebec. This offer is limited to one order per household. Not valid for current subscribers to Harlequin Desire books. All orders subject to credit approval. Credit or debit balances in a customer's account(s) may be offset by any other outstanding balance owed by or to the customer. Please allow 4 to 6 weeks for delivery. Offer available while quantities last.

**Your Privacy**—The Reader Service is committed to protecting your privacy. Our Privacy Policy is available online at www.ReaderService.com or upon request from the Reader Service.

We make a portion of our mailing list available to reputable third parties that offer products we believe may interest you. If you prefer that we not exchange your name with third parties, or if you wish to clarify or modify your communication preferences, please visit us at www.ReaderService.com/consumerchoice or write to us at Reader Service Preference Service, P.O. Box 9062, Buffalo, NY 14240-9062. Include your complete name and address.

HD15

## SPECIAL EXCERPT FROM

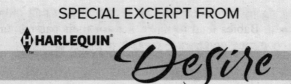

HARLEQUIN Desire

*When Brooke becomes pregnant after a one-night stand
with a sexy rancher, she tracks him down to discover
he's a widower struggling with toddler twins! Can she
help as his nanny before falling in love—and delivering
her baby bombshell?*

*Read on for a sneak peek of*
**TWINS FOR THE TEXAN**
*the latest book by* USA TODAY *bestselling author*
**Charlene Sands** *in the bestselling*
**BILLIONAIRES AND BABIES** *series*

Grateful to have made it without getting lost, Brooke had
to contend with the fact she was *here*. And now, one way
or another, her life was going to change forever. She rang
the doorbell. A moment later, she stood face-to-face with
Wyatt.

Who was holding a squirming baby boy.

It was the last thing she expected.

"Wyatt?" She was rendered speechless, staring at the
man who'd made her insides quiver just one month ago.

"Come in, Brooke. I'm glad you made it."

She stared at him, still not believing what she was
seeing. He'd never mentioned having a child. Although,
there'd seemed to be a silent agreement between them
not to delve too deeply into their private lives.

She stepped inside and Wyatt closed the door behind
her. "This is Brett, my son. He was supposed to be

sleeping by the time you arrived. Obviously that didn't happen. Babies tend to make liars of their parents, and it's been rough without a nanny."

"He's beautiful."

"Thanks, he's the best part of me. Well, him and his twin, Brianna."

*"There's two of them?"*

"I want to explain. Why don't you have a seat?" He started walking and she followed. "You look pretty, by the way," he said, his cowboy charm taking hold again, and she had trouble remembering how he'd dumped her after a spectacular night of sex.

A night when they'd conceived a child.

"You didn't tell me you had children."

"I just wanted to be me—not a father, not a widower—that night. My friends are forever saying I need to find myself again. That's what I was trying to do."

She inhaled a sharp breath, everything becoming clear.

If she were brave, she'd reveal her pregnancy to Wyatt and try to cope with the decisions they would make together. But her courage failed her. How could she tell this widower with twins he was about to be a father again?

*Don't miss*
*TWINS FOR THE TEXAN*
*by* USA TODAY *bestselling author Charlene Sands*
*available May 2016 wherever*
*Harlequin® Desire books and ebooks are sold.*

www.Harlequin.com

HDEXP0416R

*9167*

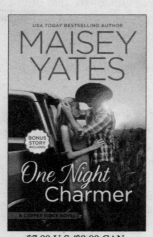

## EXCLUSIVE
## Limited time offer!

### $1.⁰⁰ OFF

*USA TODAY* Bestselling Author
## MAISEY YATES
Copper Ridge, Oregon's favorite
bachelor is about to meet his match in

*One Night*
Charmer

*Available April 19, 2016.*
*Pick up your copy today!*

$7.99 U.S./$9.99 CAN.

---

✂

### $1.⁰⁰ OFF
the purchase price of
**ONE NIGHT CHARMER by Maisey Yates.**

Offer valid from April 19, 2016, to May 31, 2016. Redeemable at participating retail outlets. Not redeemable at Barnes & Noble. Limit one coupon per purchase.
Valid in the U.S.A. and Canada only.